Flying Blind

Approach: "UK two-one-eight-three cleared for precision-monitored ILS approach to runway. You're on correct glidepath and rate of descent. Looking good."

Pilot: "Passing outer marker. Twelve hundred feet."

There were a few more moments of radio silence. Then the pilot's tone changed.

Pilot: "Approach. I've just lost direction and altitude readings."

Approach: "What? Say again."

Pilot: "I've lost all direction and altitude readings. Navigation controls dead. I've lost GPS signals. And something's blocking the localizer beam. Complete navigation system failure. Switching to manual. I'm flying blind."

Have you read?

POINT CRIME

LAWLESS & TILLEY

Flying Blind

MALCOLM ROSE

SCHOLASTIC

For Julia and Anne,
who have helped me so much

Scholastic Children's Books
Commonwealth House, 1–19 New Oxford Street,
London WC1A 1NU, UK
a division of Scholastic Ltd
London ~ New York ~ Toronto ~ Sydney ~ Auckland
Mexico City ~ New Delhi ~ Hong Kong

First published in the UK by Scholastic Ltd, 1999

Copyright © Malcolm Rose, 1999

ISBN 0 439 01070 5

Typeset by TW Typesetting, Midsomer Norton, Somerset
Printed by Cox & Wyman Ltd, Reading, Berks.

10 9 8 7 6 5 4 3 2 1

With the seat-belt lying loosely across her hips, Detective Sergeant Clare Tilley twisted awkwardly in the jumbo jet's seat, leaned towards her partner and kissed him lightly on the mouth.

"Mmm." Brett stirred, opened his eyes and said, "Nice end to a holiday."

"It's not in the manual as a way to wake up a sleeping DI but it worked. It won't happen again, though." Clare pointed out of the tiny window at the drab maze of English streets and estates like a child's intricate layout. "Look. We're nearly home. A bit different from Tobago." She tried to sound upbeat but didn't quite make it.

"Nearly back to normal," Brett commented. Detective Inspector Lawless's tone was heavy with regret. He let out a long weary breath.

Clare nodded.

In the distance, a ribbon of motorway and dual carriageways tied up Heathrow airport in a bow.

Suddenly, the aeroplane lurched, plunging and changing course unexpectedly. Their seats seemed to disappear beneath them. There was a split-second delay before their bodies caught up with the abrupt change of direction of the aircraft. Their stomachs churned unpleasantly. It was like a drastic roller-coaster ride in free-fall but it wasn't fun. It was life or death. Somewhere behind the South Yorkshire detectives, two frightened passengers let out loud, unearthly screams and several others clutched their seats, their travelling companions, their stomachs or their sick bags. The overwhelming sense of fear and impending disaster had got the better of them.

Out of the window, a smaller plane rose up into view, alarmingly near, about a couple of hundred metres away. To Brett it looked like a silvery fish, perhaps a predator shark, flashing past in a clear blue sea. A second later, it had gone. The plane had climbed high above them. Immediately, Brett and Clare both realized that the brief encounter was un-foreseen and very dangerous. It should never have happened.

The pilot's slightly shaken voice said, "Sorry about that. Everything's perfectly OK. We're con-tinuing our normal descent into Heathrow. We had to make an adjustment for another aircraft that encroached on our air space for a moment. There's nothing to worry about and no risk. We're cleared for touch down in just a couple of minutes."

Brett and Clare looked at each other. They knew instantly that the pilot was playing down the near miss. Their kiss was very nearly their last taste of life. "Phew," Brett breathed. "That was close."

Clare fell back into her seat and, still holding her midriff, murmured, "You're not kidding."

It was Saturday 30th August. On the ground, Heathrow was seething with security and police officers, including an armed response unit. Outgoing flights had been suspended. Clearly, a full-scale operation of some sort was underway but it wasn't the anti-terrorist brigade.

Brett put down his baggage, held out his warrant card to one officer and enquired, "What's going on?"

The policeman looked at the card and murmured, "South Yorkshire? Lost, are you?"

"Just on the way home," Brett replied. "And curious."

An apologetic female voice echoed around the check-in area, announcing yet more unavoidable delays.

Evasively, the officer said to Brett and Clare,

"You'll have to ask the chief if you want to find anything out."

A panicky passenger with an outlandish hat hurtled past, using his heavy suitcase as a battering ram to clear a path.

Brett stood to one side then stepped up to the policeman again. "And who's your chief?"

"DS Kosler."

"Where…?"

"Sitting with his feet up, no doubt, in the mobile control centre." He nodded towards the main exit.

Brett and Clare got a frosty reception in the police van parked outside the terminal. Detective Superintendent Dennis Kosler was too busy to be friendly. He was growling into the phone, "Yeah, it was only for thirty seconds, but in that time the planes'll fly between two and ten miles, the airport tells me. Imagine 400 tonnes of aircraft going at 600 miles an hour, two hundred passengers, and the pilot's blind-folded. It's a heavy-duty murder waiting to happen. We got away with it this time – a couple of near-misses – but I still need more people on the case." He hesitated, frowning at the newcomers, and then added, "OK. Every little helps, I suppose." He slammed down the phone and examined Brett, Clare, their luggage and their warrant cards. "Lawless, eh? What's it got to do with you?" he muttered.

"We were nearly among the victims, coming back from Tobago."

"Tobago? They pay you too much in South Yorks.

I suggest you head straight home."

"I'd like to know why we were nearly killed. I reckon you owe us that."

Dennis shrugged. "OK," he said grudgingly. Rattling off his words, he explained, "I've got a blackmailer asking for half a million quid not to knock out GPS signals. You know about GPS?"

"Global Positioning System, used to guide aircraft – and walkers in the Peak District."

"Very good," Dennis said with a sneer. "He just gave us a thirty-second demonstration to show he's serious. That's what shook you up. While he operated a gadget that jams GPS, all air traffic near Heathrow, Gatwick, Stansted, London City and Luton airports lost navigation. That's one recipe for chaos. Your plane only dodged the other because it's got a TCAS alarm, see?"

"TCAS?"

"Traffic Collision Avoidance System. It tells pilots if they're near to colliding with another plane."

Clare asked, "Does it tell them if they're going to collide with anything else – like the ground?"

"No," Dennis answered abruptly.

"Are you going to pay him off, this blackmailer?" she said.

"It's a lot of cash. What do you think, Sergeant Tilley?"

"You're not."

"He'd take the half million and then ask for more or the jammer goes back on."

Brett nodded. "Any idea who he is?"

Shaking his head, Dennis said, "We call him Strawberry."

"Strawberry?"

"My least favourite jam," he replied with grim humour. Then he announced, "Anyway, I've got heavy-duty work to do, see?"

"Fair enough," Clare said. "I'm glad it's not our baby. We're not on call until we reach the Yorkshire frontier. Even then, we might avoid work till Monday if we're really lucky."

On his way out, Brett said, "All the best with Strawberry."

"Plum assignment," Clare added with a grin.

Monday morning. After Sunday's downpours, the grass was lush and green. Strawberry stood against a tree and surveyed the park while he fingered the battery-driven contraption in his trouser pocket. It was a normal, peaceful scene with only a couple of joggers slapping their feet into the remaining puddles on the tarmac path. To Strawberry's left, a man was trimming a hedge diligently but without great skill. "Cop," Strawberry guessed. A little old lady was sitting on a bench near the rubbish bin where he'd told Dennis Kosler to leave the money. At a distance, Strawberry wasn't sure about the woman. "Probably not," he murmured to himself. On the next bench, an unshaven homeless man was sprawled, apparently dead to the world. "Definitely a cop." By the lake, a tall young man with broad shoulders was feeding the ducks and swans with bread but not many of the birds were interested in his titbits. He'd probably been throwing crusts for half an hour because he was a policeman, waiting for the extortionist to show. In the meantime, the ducks had had their fill. Now, he was trying to force-feed them till they were fat enough for the Chinese restaurant round the corner. Strawberry grinned. At least three police officers were in position, loitering to witness who picked up the ransom money.

The area would be bristling with video cameras as well. Strawberry fixed his eye on a brand new nesting box attached to the tree nearest the bin. That would be the prime site for a surveillance camera. There were probably several others as well. At the edge of the park, no doubt Detective Superintendent Dennis Kosler was sitting in a police van watching the video pictures and maintaining radio contact with all of his operatives on the ground. Strawberry knew police methods. He had seen it all on television. He had disguised himself again in case he got caught on camera but he didn't expect to be so careless. After all, he was there only to play the game of cops and robbers. He had no intention of making a bid for the bundle in the rubbish bin. Kosler had agreed to pay up too easily. He hadn't even asked for time to get the money together – as if he could take it from petty cash or walk into a bank early on Monday morning and ask for five hundred thousand pounds. The money was almost certainly counterfeit or marked in some way and the package would carry a bug so that the police could follow him. How naïve! Kosler must think he was stupid or something. No, Strawberry had come to the park only to taunt the detectives. To convince them that he was no fool.

Besides, he wasn't ready to bring the affair to an end. He had not yet finished tormenting the aviation authorities.

There was an easy way of finding out which of the people in the London park were police officers. All of them would be wired and wearing hidden earpieces so they could report developments and listen to updates from the big chief. Strawberry smiled. The electronic gadget that he had made would send an unbearable ear-splitting howl into every headphone speaker within fifty metres. He was in no hurry to activate it, though. Sure, he was eager to rattle their brain cells but somehow it was just as pleasurable to make them wait. Lingering playfully over the execution gave him a warm feeling of power and superiority. He imagined the messages that would be whizzing through the air. "Have you got a sighting yet?" "Plenty of people out for a stroll. He could be any of them. Over." "Any heading for the bin?" "Yes, there's an old... No, he's gone past." "There's a man walking his Labrador. He's sniffing the bin. The dog, that is. Now, he's off in the opposite direction. False alarm." "Female jogger headed this way. Wait. Maybe. No. She's not stopping."

Strawberry decided to put them out of their

misery. It was time to win the game. With glee, he pushed the button in his pocket.

The little old lady was the first to stand up and tear the earpiece from her head. She was far more agile than the elderly woman who she was pretending to be. The homeless man nearly fell off his bench in shock and pain. The big bloke bothering the birds nearly keeled over and squashed a couple of ducks. But the man trimming the hedge simply carried on, not aware of the silent panic around him.

Strawberry smiled. OK, he'd got it wrong, but not very wrong. He'd hoped for more entertainment than the unimaginative Kosler could provide. Perhaps Kosler would be sacked and Strawberry would get a more worthy opponent.

Strawberry's good mood suddenly evaporated. He didn't want Kosler's tainted money. He insisted on respect – so much respect that the law wouldn't dare to underestimate him ever again. He wanted half a million *without* strings attached. The money was important to him but the thing that mattered even more was having the power to make them hand over such an immense sum. Immediately, he decided to double the stakes. That would show the police that he was deadly serious. His awesome ability to bring down aircraft was worth every penny. Half a million. A million. More. Soon, they'd be begging him to accept their money. That sort of dominance sent a thrilling shiver through his spine.

Next time, Kosler – or hopefully someone more

competent – would be in the mood to obey instructions and cut out the irritating see-through tricks.

Anyway, it wasn't merely a matter of respect, money and power. Not by a long way. Strawberry had not yet had his fill of navigational jamming because he had another purpose, another motive. He still had a point to make.

DS Dennis Kosler of Thames Valley Police had agreed to pay off the extortionist that he'd code-named Strawberry. But he wasn't cleared to use real money. The bait in the bin was fake and it carried a tiny transmitter. But Strawberry hadn't fallen for it. Plainly, he was devious, resourceful and ruthless. And he was still on the loose.

One of Kosler's team, parked in front of a computer, called, "E-mail's come in, sir. You won't like it but you'll want to see it."

Dennis leaned across Stan and read from the screen: *Pathetic, Kosler. A schoolmaster would say: D–Could do better. You saturated the ground with cops and I bet the money was dirty and bugged. This time, your tactics were so transparent, I could not be bothered to prove it. Do bear in mind for the future, though, that I have a scanner. You use a transmitter of any sort and I will find it. I could physically destroy it, jam it or send it to Australia in a parcel. So, be a good boy and behave yourself. Now, you obviously need a lesson. Here is your punishment. Soon, I will use my navigational blocker for five minutes near a small airport. I will tell you for free the jammer has got a range of 50 miles. All aircraft in that range will lose their bearings completely. They will have to fly blind unless they can land but do not be surprised if I have a trick up my sleeve. I know all about Landing Systems, Localizer beams and their weaknesses. Crashes, bumpy rides and bumpy landings ahead. How many passengers will be killed? Possibly none, possibly five hundred. It is hard to predict but that is the fun of it. Whatever happens, it is all your fault, Kosler. Do not double-cross me again. I will return to Heathrow/Gatwick/Stansted/Luton again and you will be in a more co-operative mood. The price has gone up to a million. Message understood, I hope. Over and out.*

Annoyed, Dennis hissed, "Where did this come from?"

"Well," his officer answered, "it *seems* to have come from a double-glazing company but that's just a front. He's laid a false trail, re-routing it to hide its real origin. You're not going to nail him from this message."

"Damn! He's on the ball, this madman."

Stan replied, "Mad maybe, but very clever."

Dennis nodded slowly. "A dangerous combination."

It was Tuesday 2nd September. John Macfarlane looked at his officers and said, "I hope you two behaved yourselves in Tobago."

Brett and Clare glanced at each other innocently and then chimed in unison, "Us? Of course, sir."

"Mmm." Now he held the rank of Detective Chief Superintendent, John had a large desk to separate him from his detectives and a mug of proper coffee rather than a plastic cup of dubious brown liquid. No more burnt fingers and tortured taste buds for him. Yet, if he could, he would give it all up to get back out there into the real world and do real detective work again. "The West Indian authorities seem pleased with the advice you were able to give."

"We might be called back to give evidence when the case goes to trial," Clare responded. She kept a straight face but really she was teasing the chief.

"That," Big John said emphatically, "sounds like a serious skive to me. If they really can't do without your testimony, we'll set up a video link." He grinned and added, "Nice try, though. But the charms of Sheffield will have to do for the moment." Still talking to Clare, he commented, "You look relaxed and even a little bit tanned." He sipped some coffee. "Obviously, the break's done you both good but it's back to the grind now."

"What have you got for us?" asked Brett.

"Nothing major, but there's a whole load of routine stuff to deal with." He pushed a folder towards them. "Oh, you might as well look into this as well." He handed them a piece of paper from the fax machine. "It's just come in."

Brett took one look at it and smiled at the coincidence. The note had come from Dennis Kosler and it had been sent to every force with an airport on its patch. The message was a warning that a blackmailer code-named Strawberry might disrupt a small airport with a device that jammed navigational signals. The faxed memo included instructions on accessing Thames Valley's full case notes through the on-line police computer.

Brett admitted, "We know all about this. Our plane nearly crashed into another one on the approach to Heathrow. The pilot had to take evasive action."

"And how," Clare said. "My stomach's only just got back where it should be."

"It's just the job for you, then," John said. "Besides, it looks like serious electronics and science stuff. That's right up your street, Brett. But unless you get a whiff that this Strawberry's operating in South Yorkshire, it's low priority. OK?"

Gathering up the paperwork, they said in chorus, "OK."

Suspicious, Big John leaned forward and muttered, "You two look far too happy and ... cosy. We'll soon put that right now you're back."

"How was Tobago, then?" Phil Chapman asked.

"Sunny. Gorgeous. Laid back," Brett replied.

With a roguish grin, Phil said, "And how was Clare?"

"A touch sunburnt but she enjoyed it."

Phil took up his pint and, before taking a sip, said, "That's not what I meant – and you know it."

"He's not going to tell us the juicy bits," said Shaun.

On Tuesday evening, Brett and a couple of friends were enjoying a chat in the pub. His mates were feeling disgruntled because they'd only been hiking in the Peak District while Brett had been sunning himself in the West Indies.

Brett changed the subject. "How were the hills?"

"Good," Phil said. "If you hadn't been spoiling yourself in the tropics, you'd have enjoyed tramping through the Peaks."

"True."

"Yeah," Shaun put in. Clearly wanting to bait Phil, he said, "Maybe Brett could've been navigator."

"You're not going to let me forget about that, are you?"

"Did you get lost or something?" Brett asked.

"Phil here has got an expensive, posh person's compass," Shaun replied with a smile. "No matter where you are, it'll tell you. And it'll plot a path back to where you started. It's impossible to get lost so, no, we don't need an old-fashioned thing with its silly unreliable needle pointing north." He joked, "We have a hi-tech, digital, radio-controlled, genetically modified, can't-possibly-go-wrong bit of new technology."

"What happened?"

"Three hundred quid well spent. It went wrong."

Phil shrugged. "Don't look at me. It should've worked perfectly. There was nothing wrong with it. Before you ask, the batteries were fine and we weren't near any RAF base where the military scrambles the signals. It just refused to give us position readings sometimes."

Suddenly, Brett was aware that their conversation might be relevant to his case. "This thing's based on GPS signals, is it?"

"Not another technology freak!" Shaun moaned.

Phil nodded. "It's brilliant. There's a network of satellites that broadcast radio signals. A hand-held navigator picks up the GPS beams and uses them to calculate exactly where it is. It's got an accuracy of fifteen metres but if you get an expert to tinker with the circuitry, it can give you pinpoint accuracy. It can tell you where you are to within one centimetre! Latitude, longitude, OS map, obstacles, route maps, how fast you're moving, it tells you the lot."

"That's if it works at all," Shaun muttered.

"Why didn't it work?" Brett said.

"No idea."

"Was it like someone was jamming the satellite signals so it couldn't receive them at all?"

"Yes. That'd knock it out. And it makes sense," Phil said. "I heard the radio signals are pretty weak. I'm no expert but I'd guess that'd make them easy to jam – with the right equipment." Quizzically, Phil looked at Brett and asked, "Do you know something I don't about GPS navigation?"

"I'm not sure," Brett answered hesitantly. "Possibly. I *do* know someone's got a jammer and used it recently down south. I can't say what for. It's a long shot but I guess he could have had a little practice up here first and interfered with your position indicator. When exactly did it go on the blink?"

"The weekend before last. Three times I noticed it on the Saturday – that'd be the 23rd – and at least twice on the Sunday."

"Morning or afternoon?"

"Both."

Shaun put down his drink and said, "You'd better crack on and arrest this man with the jammer, Brett, before the hills are alive with lost hikers."

Phil did not joke about it. He had reasoned that there was much more at stake than a few wayward walkers.

Tuesday was about to turn into Wednesday and Brett felt curiously detached. But it wasn't that curious. Not really. For two and a half weeks, he'd shared his life with Clare in the West Indies. For that time, they had not been apart. They had even shared a room at the hotel. Now, she was on the other side of town. It could have been the other side of the world. He wondered what she was doing. Out with friends? Female friends or male friends? At home with a beer? Asleep?

Brett was taking a long luxurious bath, unable to clear his head of thoughts of Clare and the relationship that had nearly evolved between them in Tobago. Maybe one day, when they weren't the Lawless and Tilley team any more, their partnership could develop some more. An image came to his mind of a sad empty table in the corner of a busy restaurant. The notice on the table read *Reserved* but the diners had not yet turned up.

Clare showed her warrant card to the walkers as she mingled with them on Wednesday morning at the start of the Pennine Way in Edale village. Brett was trawling Edale's camp sites and car parks. He watched out for the ramblers with off-road vehicles, the best water-proof gear and pricey boots who might also own GPS navigators. Then he went up to them and talked about the joys of hill-walking, the joys of modern gadgets.

Meeting afterwards in the pub, Brett and Clare compared notes. Brett had found a group of hikers who were out trekking on 23rd and 24th August with a position indicator. Clare had questioned a solitary male walker who also owned one and was backpacking through the Peaks at the same time as Phil and Shaun. And, yes, they *had* noticed that their GPS navigators had let them down occasionally at various points along the route. So, it wasn't just Phil's new toy that was intermittently faulty. Something had disrupted the satellite radio signals. Brett felt pleased that he had a lead. He had something to take back to John so he could press for the investigation to be stepped up. He fancied taking on such an unusual and intriguing case. "But first," he said to Clare, "let's not waste an opportunity. We're here now. How about lunch? We can take it outside on the grass."

"And pretend we're still in Tobago?" she said.

"Relax, enjoy."

"No hurry."

Clare laughed. "Not till we get back into the swing of English inquiries. Then it's twenty-four hours a day."

Back at headquarters, Big John listened to them and then complained, "It's a bit tenuous. You've got a few dodgy GPS signals, for sure, but no evidence it's down to Strawberry and no evidence he's going to target Sheffield's shiny new airport."

"True," Brett admitted. "But we don't know any other reason for these navigators to go wrong, so it could well have been Strawberry. It'd mean he's from round here or he's used Derbyshire and South Yorkshire for testing his jammer. That's surely worth looking into."

John sighed. "OK. I agree. It's not much to go on but the threat's so dire, you'd better check it out. Get on to this Dennis Kosler and let him know what you're up to, and get on-line to his latest info."

"Personnel?" Brett prompted.

"I haven't got a lot of slack in the system. It'll be the two of you plus a researcher. That's all. Now…"

Brett and Clare knew what lay behind John's hesitation. The boss would have assigned Liz Payn. He was missing her expertise and irreverent humour.

"I haven't been able to replace Liz yet," he said in a sombre tone. "As if it's possible to replace someone like her."

"There's always Louise Jenson," Brett suggested.

"Jenson?" John exclaimed. "She's still on community service."

He was joking. But he had punished her for a mistake during one of Brett's cases six weeks ago by putting her back on the beat.

Brett disagreed with John's tactics. He felt that the young officer needed the confidence of her superiors, not a reprimand. She had the makings of a fine assistant if only she was given the opportunities and experience.

"I'll take responsibility for her," Brett said. "Won't we, Clare?"

Reluctantly, Clare nodded.

John let out a long breath. "Well, I must admit, I'm seriously stuck for support otherwise." He hesitated, still unwilling to reassign Jenson, but then caved in. "All right. Her tutor sergeant's been sending in good reports on her. Personally, I think it's too early for the girl. I don't think she's ready but I don't have a lot of choice." He fixed his eyes on Brett and said, "Since you're so keen to enlist her, it's your shout, Brett. I'll hold you to that responsibility. She's on probation with you. Let's hope she doesn't become a liability. Just make sure she doesn't slip up again."

"I'll keep an eye on her. She'll be fine."

As a parting shot, John said, "Just remember, between the three of you, you've got fewer service years than the cleaner who does this room. That's a cocktail capable of real disaster. Watch what you're doing."

It wasn't much of an incident room. It was a poky little office with two rusty filing cabinets, a fax and phone, a tiny table, and a couple of computers. Still, there was a drinks machine right outside in the corridor. Brett and Clare knew that, until Strawberry turned up on the doorstep and threatened Sheffield City Airport, the case deserved no more.

Brett spread out his arms and said, "Welcome to the incident cupboard."

Louise giggled and then turned serious. "Brett. Clare. I want to thank you for … you know … giving me…"

Interrupting, Brett said, "No need, Louise. We asked for you because we think you're the best person for the job, not to do you a favour. Have you read the case notes yet?"

Louise could never be faulted for her diligence. She nodded.

"Well, I see it like this. First, we assume Strawberry and his jammer were responsible for the position indicators refusing to work in the Peaks. If that's right, what are the options? Maybe Strawberry was in these parts the weekend before last and now he's gone. In that case, our job's to find out all we can about him and his visit, and pass the info to Kosler. We assist and that's that. But maybe Strawberry's based up here. That way, we're the ones to catch him before he threatens any air traffic anywhere. There's another possibility. Maybe he's about to have a go at Sheffield airport. That puts us in the front line with a vested interest in arresting him before he brings a plane down on our patch."

Clare smiled. "Be honest, Brett. You'd like him to be here, wouldn't you? You like the idea of this one."

"He's a lot more interesting than your average South Yorkshire crook – and he beats everything in John's folder of routine cases."

Louise felt pressured. Detective Chief Superintendent John Macfarlane had made it abundantly clear that she was under test. He'd told her that Brett and Clare would be judging her every step of the way. And he'd reminded her of Lawless and Tilley's reputation. Their success rate made them the most effective detectives in South Yorkshire Police. Macfarlane did not want her to be responsible for tarnishing their enviable record. She told herself that the investigation was very different from the Chapman case but she saw a worrying parallel. Again, someone was demanding a ransom. Last time a little girl, Phil Chapman's daughter, had been the pawn. This time, it was every aeroplane passenger. Last time, Louise had fouled it up. She glanced at Clare's bare right arm and saw the ugly scar that was one result of her mistake. A constant reminder of her failure was written permanently on Clare's arm. This time, Louise was determined not to mess it up. She tilted her head to one side while she listened to Brett and Clare.

"OK," Brett said. "Assuming he's on our patch or at least has been, how are we going to get him? Louise?"

"Find out who he is," she replied rather lamely.

"Yes," Brett said. "There's a bit of wall space up there. Let's have a sheet of paper up, split into columns. It'll be our word-picture of Strawberry. Label the first column *Identity/appearance*. Clare? Suggestions?"

Clare said, "Not *who* he is but *why* he's doing it."

"You would say that," Brett said with a smile. "Always into people's brains and motivations. So, call the second column *Motive*. It's got to be more than money. Jamming GPS signals is too out of the ordinary to be just a money-making scheme. What else? There's the where as well as the who and why. Never mind who he is and why he's doing it, we'd get him if we knew exactly where he is, so let's have

Location in the third column."

Louise was jotting down notes on her pad. Nervously, she looked up and added, "If you're right, he gets around a bit. You know, he's been up here and down in London. Perhaps we should target his car or whatever he's got."

Brett nodded. "True. Let's make a fourth column. Just label it *Other* – for odds and ends as well as any vehicle details. Now, we need a print-out of everything Thames Valley's got. Establish the link with them, will you, Louise? Then we can use their data to start putting a few things in our columns. I don't like to see an empty piece of paper. There's always something we know. Straightaway, we can guess he's into electronics in a big way. That goes under *Identity*. We think he tested his jammer within fifty miles of the moors above Kinder Scout. That's an entry for *Location*."

Clare said, "And in the *Motive* column you can write *Possible grudge against airlines?*"

The door opened and Detective Sergeant Mark Yelland strolled in. "Mmm. Cosy incident room," he remarked. Before they could reply, he said, "Clare, Brett. I've got a little job for you."

"Oh? What's that?"

"I'm putting together a quiz team. We've got a challenge coming up next Monday with a bunch of lawyers and a team from the university. Give the lawyers half a chance and they'll cheat."

With a grin, Brett said, "I see. You want us to investigate the lawyers?"

"Very funny. No. I need volunteers and you're them."

"Well, we're just starting a case…"

Looking round the lowly room, he said, "It's not exactly high profile, is it? Anyway, you two are ideal. Brett, you'll be able to answer all the science stuff, and Clare, you're unbeatable on art and literature. On top of that, you're both into sport so you'll be able to field those questions between you."

Clare smiled and shook her head. "What about history, geography and all the rest?"

"There's four in each team – like University Challenge. I've got someone from Fraud who's hot on history – and a film buff, which helps. And I'll slaughter 'em on geography. I had a holiday in Switzerland once. Come on. It's happening on Monday at seven and it'll only be for an hour, if that. You've got to do it. It's all for charity and Yorkshire TV said they'll cover it. It'll be a better chance for stardom than your usual press conference."

Brett and Clare looked at each other and shrugged. Clare said, "OK. We'll do it. We agree to make fools of ourselves."

Clare waved the hardcopy of Strawberry's e-mail message to Dennis Kosler and said, "Here's your most interesting document so far, Brett."

"Why's that?"

"Some of these sentences stick out a mile, like, 'A schoolmaster would say: D- Could do better.'

Strawberry's playing with us." Both Brett and Louise looked over Clare's shoulder as she pointed out the passage. "For one thing, he uses the term, 'schoolmaster'. When did you last hear that? Ages ago, I'll bet. What does it suggest to you?"

"An old independent school," Brett said. "Or maybe a grammar school."

"Right," Clare said. "And this thing about a D-grade. I bet it applies to Strawberry. I think he's got a chip on his shoulder about a teacher who gave him low grades. He's obviously bright so I smell hostility there. He might be a disaffected ex-pupil of an independent school."

"You said he was toying with us. Perhaps he's trying to lead us up the garden path," Brett replied. "Maybe he only ever got A grades and he got on perfectly well at school."

Clare disagreed. "If he hasn't got a thing about school, why's he written a lot in school terms? *Be a good boy and behave yourself. Now, you obviously need a lesson. Here's your punishment.* And why would he quote this D-? No, he's got a hang up of some sort. He might have a thing about authority."

"And a thing about revenge." Accepting his partner's opinion, Brett added, "I suppose if his cleverness wasn't recognized at school, he might hold a grudge. That'd explain the tone of the message. Now, he's certainly got a grudge against Kosler and wants to punish him. He's hooked on revenge, maybe."

"So why target aircraft?" Louise asked. "What's he getting revenge for?"

Clare shrugged. "Was one of his flights delayed, do you reckon?"

Brett laughed. "It'd have to be a long delay to make someone that mad. Anyway," he said to Louise, "get on to independent, boarding and grammar schools, first near here then spread out. It's a long shot but we want details of all unhappy students who eventually came good in physics and electronics, any known feuds with a male physics teacher. That sort of thing."

Rather startled at the prospect, Louise said, "That's a big job."

"Let's get stuck in, then."

"Just one thing first," Louise said.

"Yes?"

"We're all saying 'he', but is Strawberry a man?"

"Good point," Clare responded. "But everything smells of a male. Electronics, threats, the tone of the e-mail. Kosler had a profiler look over everything. Conclusion? Yeah, it's a man."

"I know," Louise said, "but there's no real proof."

Brett smiled. "You sound just like me. You'll believe it's definitely a man when Forensic's isolated a Y chromosome. But this time," he said, "even I think it's a he. All his communication's got a male ring to it. You're right to bring it up, Louise, but let's crack on under the assumption Strawberry's male – unless we get any evidence to the contrary. We check out the most obvious and likely theory and only come up with another if we prove the first one's wrong."

"Right," Louise said, one hand already reaching for the phone. With the other, she turned on one of the computers.

In the Technology Department of the university, Professor Naoki Matsumoto was playing with his pet cockroach. The electronically modified insect – a half-robot, half-cockroach called Robotroach or Robbie for short – was crawling slowly through a maze. At each corner, Robbie hesitated, swivelled round to take pictures with the miniature video camera on his back-pack, and then made a decision about which way to go. Naoki did not intervene by giving him electronic instructions about the correct direction.

With a little nod of the head, the Japanese expert in electronics shook Brett's hand vigorously and warmly and then did the same to Clare, asking her if the injury on her arm had cleared up. Then he said enthusiastically, "Look." He pointed at the maze. For a minute, they watched Robbie negotiate another corner.

"You're not controlling him," Brett noted.

"Exactly. I'm making lots of improvements," Naoki boasted. "I've added artificial intelligence software. He's learning for himself how to get to the food at the other side of the maze. After a couple of fact-finding trips, he'll go straight through without mistakes. All thanks to you."

"Us?"

"After I helped you – after Robbie helped you – with your kidnap case, I secured a lot of extra research funding. I'm using it to add artificial intelligence and develop a better heat-seeking camera for him. That will allow him to learn to seek out body warmth within collapsed buildings. He'll be much more effective at finding earthquake survivors."

"Sounds good," Brett said.

"You want him for another investigation?" Naoki asked hopefully.

"No, not this time. We're after a different sort of advice: your knowledge of electronics. We wanted to ask you about Global Positioning Systems and, in particular, jamming them."

"Ah, yes," Naoki replied. "I know what you mean but it's not my field. You want to speak to my colleague, Dr Tim Darke. His office is just around the corner. He's a specialist in radio and radar signals. He knows all about GPS. And he's in right now, preparing for the new term."

"OK. We'll have a chat with him. Thanks. And good luck with Robbie."

With a sly twinkle in his eye, Naoki said, "Tim's not been so lucky as me with research funding. Perhaps if you can use him like you used me, his research might get a boost as well. Very good."

Brett laughed. "We'll see what we can do. No promises, though."

Tim was sitting at his desk, tapping on a keyboard,

surrounded by cluttered book shelving and shabby filing cabinets. He was in his thirties, dressed in jeans and sweatshirt, and he looked fed up. Obviously pleased to take a break, he explained, "For my sins, I teach the computing part of the undergraduate course. Just awful. Computer technology moves so fast, what I taught last year's bunch is way out of date. I have to rewrite the course every year. It's a pain. Anyway, enough of my whingeing, what can I do for South Yorkshire Police?"

"Naoki said you could tell us all about GPS."

Tim nodded. "Correct." He lingered over the r sound so that the word came out as *caw-wrecked*. "It's a navigation system – not the best method one could imagine, and pity it's American-owned – but it's still pretty good. What do you want to know about it?"

"It's more about jamming GPS signals than GPS itself."

"Oh?"

Brett did not want to tell the university lecturer too much. "Someone out there has got hold of a jamming device and could cause a bit of havoc."

"To say the least," Tim said, sitting up straight and suddenly interested. "It's a lot more than a bit. Do you know what that could do to air traffic?"

Brett nodded. "And so does he, I'm afraid."

"A terrorist, presumably."

Brett would not be drawn on detail. "Possibly," he answered. "But what would you need to make one?"

"Me? I wouldn't want to make one at all."

"No, I meant, what would a terrorist need? Lots of money and expertise?"

Tim Darke thought about it for a moment and cast a discreet, admiring glance at Clare. "Not that much. You see, satellites can't carry huge power packs or they'd drop out of the sky, so they can only generate weak signals. It's a big, big drawback. That's why GPS is vulnerable to jamming. And that's why I said it's not the best imaginable system. It wouldn't be very expensive, difficult or arduous to make a jammer. Come into my lab for a second – or at least the poky place the university laughingly calls my lab."

Brett and Clare followed the lecturer down the corridor and into another room. It was windowless and dust-free, long and narrow with a smooth bench down one side. There were four computers spaced evenly along the work surface and three students sitting next to them, several chips and boards lying on the bench. Underneath the work surface there were several metal cabinets with grey sliding drawers. No doubt, they were used to store electronic components. Behind the students, the shelves clinging to the other wall were crammed with more electronic parts.

Tim said, "If I put these research students on a project to make a GPS jammer, they'd simply get on the Internet, find out everything about building one from a dodgy website, and then construct one in this very room. It's just a matter of broadcasting electrical noise at the same frequencies used for GPS and receivers won't be able to lock on to the proper signals. That's not a very tough task. The theory was published a few years ago in a Russian science journal called *Radioteknika*. Even these layabouts would have it made in a week – two at the outside – and I'd hardly notice the hole it'd make in the departmental budget. A few hundred pounds, a thousand at the outside. Most of the equipment they'd need would be in a lab like this."

"And if it wasn't? Where would they go to buy the electronic bits and pieces they'd need?"

"There aren't that many suppliers left now. Again, you could order stuff through the Internet from various virtual shops. Round here, though, you'd go to Electrics Unlimited in Attercliffe. That's about your lot."

One of the research students, a young woman wearing hefty walking boots called Vanessa Street, turned round and remarked, "Actually, if our grants would stretch to it, we could just buy a jammer and save all the bother. I've seen them advertised on the Internet – a Russian site – for four thousand dollars. If I remember rightly it was a company called Aviaconversia. Of course, we get peanuts for a grant," she said aggressively, "so we couldn't afford one, even if we wanted one for some reason."

"And it's illegal to test or use a device like that in the UK and most other western countries," Tim put in.

Back in Dr Darke's office, Brett said, "Your research students have got degrees in electronics,

I guess. Is that the level of person we're looking for?"

"Probably," Tim answered as he sat back down on his swivel chair. "But not necessarily. There are some pretty good self-taught amateurs in this game. They're the sort of people who got a do-it-yourself radio kit for Christmas when they were kids. Their mums and dads probably hoped making their own simple radios would keep them quiet, thinking they'd never do it, but they did. It didn't keep them quiet at all. Then they got encouraged by their success, inspired by getting their own crackly radio reception. They went on to become cleaners, stock-brokers, vicars, actors, but they kept up an interest in electronics. That sort of person could do it, no problem."

"Have you just got the three research students?" Clare asked.

He smiled at her. "Correct. My funds won't let me take on more, unfortunately."

"I'd better take their names," she said.

"I don't think they're the type... They wouldn't jeopardize their careers."

"No, but they could be useful contacts."

"All right." Keeping his eyes on Clare, Tim dictated his postgraduate students' names for her. As he spoke, he swayed slightly in his mobile chair. His trousers had ridden up slightly, revealing that the lecturer was wearing odd socks: one black and one white.

"What size would this jammer be?" Brett enquired.

"I don't know for sure," Tim answered. "I've never seen one. But there's nothing inherently big in it. The bulkiest bit would probably be a battery pack, like a laptop computer, but the jammer would only consume a few watts. I bet the whole thing would probably be laptop size – or even a bit smaller."

"So it'd fit into a holdall or briefcase?"

"Correct," he replied in his exaggerated way. "Or a computer carrier case."

"That's probably about it for the moment," Brett said. "Thanks a lot. You've been very helpful. If we have any more questions, can we contact you again?"

Tim shrugged. "Why not? It beats lecture notes on PC technology."

In the early afternoon, the small electronics shop was packed. Packed with customers. Packed with rickety shelves stacked high with transistors, bulbs, chips, cables, power packs, plugs and sockets, resistors, capacitors. It had the air of a shadowy shop, as if all of the goods were illicit. It was the only place in Sheffield that sold this obscure stuff to radio enthusiasts. None of it was pre-packaged. Fuses could be bought by the fistful or singly for a few pence. It was the sort of shop that had mostly been displaced by the big DIY superstores. Yet it sold items for defunct radios, tape recorders, televisions, vacuum cleaners that had long since been abandoned as obsolete and unprofitable by those giant out-of-town stores. That's why it was crowded with devotees of unfashionable soldering irons and circuit boards. These were people who turned up their noses at modern motherboards and chips that were simply thrown out and replaced when they went wrong, who regarded modern PCs as too easy and too delicate. And, yes, several wore anoraks in case of rain.

Eventually, Brett and Clare managed to push their way to the front, past an obstinate customer wearing a Stetson hat, to see the shop manager. Like his two assistants, Dylan McPhee was wearing the uniform of a bright green T-shirt with the Electrics Unlimited logo. He was annoyed that the detectives were using up his precious time, causing an even bigger queue in the shop. The forty-year-old with distinctive silver hair took them into a back room that smelt musty. He didn't offer them seats. In fact, there was only one in the stock room. Straightaway, Brett asked if any of McPhee's customers had been in recently to buy the components needed to assemble a GPS jammer.

Interestingly, the impatient shop owner did not have to query what Brett was talking about. Plainly he knew all about the Global Positioning System and the type of device that could be constructed to jam its signals. He sighed. "I can't possibly keep track of what every customer buys," he muttered. "You saw how busy we are. They're buying all sorts, mainly to build radios and repair equipment that manufacturers have turned their backs on." He sounded distinctly agitated. "And I should be serving them."

"You look like you're doing pretty well out of it," Clare said.

"Yeah, but most of them will be spending forty-nine pence on a new resistor or a specialist fuse," Dylan replied. "That shopful will probably amount to five or ten pounds worth of sales. I'll tell you, this sort of shop is on the way out. It's not financially viable any more. I don't know what the world's coming to. Come back in a year's time, and I bet this shop won't be here. I'll be bankrupt. All my customers will be chucking out broken irons because they can't get the parts any more, or because the makers charge more to repair than to buy a new one. All for the want of a simple resistor. In case you hadn't noticed, I'm not very happy with this wasteful throw-away culture of ours."

Clare smiled. "Yes, I'd noticed. Are you sure you can't put your finger on a customer who's been buying parts that could make a jammer?"

"Well…"

"We'll let you get back to those precious customers as soon as you tell us if you've got any suspicions at all."

Dylan sniffed and then said, "I'm probably barking up the wrong tree entirely but a man called Nash has been buying some interesting stuff. I had to order a few items for him. I suppose they could go into a noise transmitter – as well as a number of other things."

"Any idea what his full name is and where he lives?"

"I don't know, but he had a local accent. He always paid cash and didn't want delivery. He didn't leave an address or telephone number. He said he'd just drop in whenever he passed to see if his order had arrived. That's what he did."

"Has he got anything on order right now?"

"No. I haven't seen him for ... I don't know ... two or three weeks."

"If he comes in again, can you give us a call? It'd be very helpful." Clare handed Dylan a card showing her name and the police telephone number.

"OK," he agreed.

"Do you have security cameras in the shop?" asked Brett.

"They're too expensive," Dylan replied.

Denied a photograph of Mr Nash, Clare took down Dylan's rough description of him. And it was very rough. The only distinguishing features that were clear in McPhee's memory were Mr Nash's glasses and moustache. Both could be standard theatrical props.

Brett and Clare fought their way through the crowd and out of the shop.

On the way to the car, Brett put out his hand to feel the drizzle that fell from a dull grey sky. "Ugh. It's not like this in Tobago."

Clare laughed. "Goodbye to warm refreshing rain, hello to the cold British stuff. We're back in Sheffield and it's nearly autumn. Floods to look forward to, then snow. Welcome home."

They piled their wet coats on top of one of the filing cabinets and Brett asked Louise, "How's your schoolwork coming on?"

Louise grimaced like someone with a migraine. "There's an awful lot of independent schools. And that's not the only problem. Because Strawberry's pretty good at electronics, he must have studied it a bit. That means his schooldays could be a few years back so I need to check out a lot of old grammar schools and the like. Quite a few of them have changed status, you know. They're under local education authority control or they've gone grant maintained or they've become some other sort. It's a nightmare. But I'm compiling a list – a very long list – and every time I put another school on it, I send a confidential memo to the Head, asking about ex-pupils in the electronics trade. There's no replies in yet. Heads seem to be busy teaching or managing or whatever they do."

"Hopefully, they're consulting with physics teachers," Brett replied. "But keep it up, Louise. We might have rescued you from the beat but we didn't promise a picnic."

Louise was a few days away from her twenty-first birthday and, measured against Brett and Clare, she seemed short and slight. She had curly fair hair that tumbled to her shoulders. She looked smart. Obviously she took considerable care over her appearance and clothing. She was lightly but carefully made up and her clothes were stylish, making the most of her slender figure. Clare guessed that she was not just trying to impress her new superiors but that she was meticulous about the way she looked. Clare smiled. Louise would put her and Brett to shame.

Louise had already written on their wall chart. *Tested jammer within 50 miles of Kinder Scout* appeared below *Location*. In the *Identity/Appearance* column, she had put *Probably male, Ex-pupil of independent school?* and *Clash with (science) schoolmaster?* Brett leaned towards the paper and, with a felt-tip, added *Professional electronics engineer?* and *Amateur radio enthusiast?* to the same column. There were a depressing number of question marks.

"I'm glad you did that," Louise remarked. "My spelling's not up to it."

"We need you to trace all local men with a name of Nash as well. Then see if any of your feedback from the schools comes up with a Nash. We'd be very interested if that happened." As Brett spoke he scrawled in the *Other* column. *Suppliers: WWW, Aviaconversia, Electrics Unlimited.*

Brett and Clare updated Louise with all of their latest information and together they made a computer catalogue. In one folder, they listed electronics experts: Tim Darke, his students and Dylan McPhee. In a second folder, they recorded the scant details of their first suspect: Mr Nash. Brett anticipated that they'd have several more entries before the end of the investigation.

Within three quarters of an hour of surfing on the other computer, Brett found the websites of Aviaconversia, a strange eastern cult based in Poland, and a group in the Middle East that seemed to be dedicated mainly to terrorizing the USA and Britain. The first offered GPS jammers for sale, the second two had pages on how to construct a GPS disrupter for use against the decadent countries of the West. "It's frighteningly easy," Brett announced. "As Vanessa Street said, four thousand dollars will buy you a jammer."

"Does that mean Strawberry might not be an electronics whiz-kid?" Louise asked. "Might he just have some cash to spare and a grudge?"

"Not when you marry it with his little digs at Kosler," Brett answered.

Clare explained, "Remember, at the drop-site, he blew a few earpieces somehow. Then, in his e-mail, he said he's got a scanner for bugs and he knows all about airport landing systems and localizer beams, whatever they are – but they sound hi-tech and important."

"Yeah. Trip to the airport next, Clare," Brett said.

"Are you offering to take me on holiday again?"

"From Sheffield?" Brett exclaimed. "It's a hut in the middle of a long narrow field. I think the only flights go to Amsterdam and Jersey."

"I could cope with either," Clare said.

"Not if Strawberry's around with his jammer."

The newly-built Sheffield City Airport was more than a hut in a field. But not a lot more. Ringed with a wire fence, two metres high, it was located just off Parkway, the major road that linked the city to the M1. The small terminal building had a white corrugated roof that overhung the glassy walls. To one side there was a scanty car park and a square air traffic control tower – more of a stump than a tower. Behind, a railway, a grubby marshalling yard and a string of giant pylons ran parallel to the single runway. Beyond the airstrip and orange windsock there was a back-cloth of trees. The rising hill of a golf course, some steel works and South Yorkshire Police Operations Complex lay at the right-hand end of the landing strip. The 15.50 flight to Amsterdam had just left. There were no other departures for the day and the last arrival from Holland was not expected until after eight o'clock. The Jersey connections flew only at weekends. With three 32-seater planes coming and going during weekdays, it was not exactly Heathrow. Outside the building, two members of staff were smoking cigarettes and chatting animatedly. Inside, the flight terminal was no more than a café area, a check-in and information desk, and an opening to the modest departure lounge.

The airport manager saw Brett and Clare in her office that overlooked the empty runway. Like every other airport manager, Danielle had already received a warning about Strawberry direct from Dennis Kosler. "As far as I can see," she said, moving a brown attaché case from the table and putting it out of sight, "there's no action I can take – other than to tell my ATC staff and safety crew to be ready for anything – unless you advise me otherwise." She sat back in her cushioned chair.

"I'm afraid I can't add much to that," Brett replied. "But your security people should be keeping an eye open for anyone lurking around the site."

"As I understand it, though," Danielle said, "this blackmailer could jam navigational signals from up to fifty miles away. Surely if he wants to play havoc with a GPS jammer, he'll make sure he isn't near the airport he's targeting. That way, he won't get caught in a security net."

"That sounds like good sense," Brett admitted, "but I still think he'll be somewhere near the bull's-eye when he turns on his jammer. Let me explain why. Are all your flights on time?"

"Ah, you heard."

"No. I was asking because I don't know."

"We're running a tighter ship than we did at first but we have a few delays – like any other means of transport. The planes are often half an hour late."

Brett replied, "OK. Now, imagine you're the blackmailer. See it from his point of view. You'd check out the flight times. Two incoming flights from Amsterdam each morning, one in the afternoon. That's all. So, not a lot of aircraft to aim at. If you're a long way away, how do you know when to flick the switch? At the scheduled time? You'd look pretty silly if the plane was half an hour late. Let's be honest, this isn't Heathrow where there'll always be a good few planes in the area to hit. I think he'd have to be near by, keeping watch or listening for a plane, then turn on the jammer."

Danielle said thoughtfully, "I see your point." She was a bit older than Brett and Clare, perhaps thirty or early thirties, and yet still young to be in charge of an organization like an airport. She was chic and attractive, wearing a suit and rimless glasses that, at a distance, were hardly visible at all.

Clare enquired, "Couldn't he keep his distance and check out travel bulletins on Teletext, Ceefax, the Internet or local radio?"

Danielle smiled wryly. "If only. Our little airport isn't quite renowned or established enough to warrant

TV coverage," she replied. "The Internet and radio aren't always reliable. They don't necessarily announce delays – for fear of putting passengers off – and when they do, they quote *expected* times of arrival. It's the same if someone phones the help desk: they get an ETA. I dare say it wouldn't be accurate enough for someone wanting to disrupt flights."

Clare nodded. Changing the subject, she asked, "What's a localizer?"

"You're looking at one." Danielle pointed out of the window at a bright yellow array of aerials that decorated the end of the runway. The antennae looked like a surrealist's model of space-age weapons. "It's part of the ILS – Instrument Landing System. It sends out a radio beam that marks the exact centre of the runway. Incoming pilots lock on to it so they know they're lined up for landing."

"Nice colour scheme."

With a grin, Danielle said, "It's yellow so pilots know what they've hit if they overshoot the runway."

Seeing the South Yorkshire Police outpost just beyond the aerials and rows of airport lights, Brett said, "Once we're done here, we'll nip round the corner to our Operations Complex. Ironic that it's on your doorstep. Anyway, we'll get them to draw up plans. We can mobilize a lot of officers around here pretty quickly."

Danielle frowned. "From the way you're speaking, it sounds as if you expect this maniac to have a go at us. Is that true?"

"No. I'm just talking contingency plans, that's all. He could strike anywhere. I should say, though, that we have reason to believe he might have connections with this area." Brett paused before adding, "Which brings me to my next point. Do you know anyone with a grudge against any airlines? Maybe employees or, more likely, ex-employees."

Uncertain, the manager answered, "Well... Not really."

Clare noticed the hesitation immediately and pounced. "But you know something. You should tell us even the slightest thing."

Danielle replied, "I was thinking we did have to lose an air traffic controller a couple of weeks back."

"Lose? How do you mean?"

Clumsily, Danielle dropped a biro. She bent down and picked it up from the lush green carpet before answering. "He had a problem – a drink problem." She took a deep breath and said, "ATC is a profession for clear heads. I have to insist on that. Safety comes first in air traffic control."

"So you had to sack him."

Danielle nodded. "He didn't think it was justified. Before he left, he said a few choice words to me. He thought I wasn't being fair so I guess there's possibly a grudge there. But it's not the sort of grudge you're after, is it? It'd be more against me than the airport business in general, I'd have thought. Still, I suppose you can never tell how someone'll react – especially if they're under the influence of alcohol."

"Exactly," Clare said. "We'll have to look into it. What's his name?"

Michael Breach owned a big house in leafy Beauchief. It overlooked Hutcliff Wood and Millhouses Park. The out-of-work air traffic controller was not at home but his wife agreed to speak to them in the spacious living room after Clare had explained, not entirely truthfully, that they were looking into the running of the ATC unit at Sheffield City Airport. Mrs Breach seemed rather malicious towards the airport and saw an opportunity to vent her feelings.

"We moved to this place," she said, spreading her hands to indicate the house, "because of Mike's new job. Then what happens – almost as soon as we've unpacked the boxes? Just because Mike enjoys a few off-duty beers – who doesn't? – he's out of work. Do you know how many openings there are for an air traffic controller in Sheffield? Roughly zero. Without Mike working, bringing in a regular salary, we can't afford the mortgage on this house. It'll be re-possessed sooner or later. Then where will we be? On the streets. I've got a baby asleep in the next room. What's going to become of him?"

"So a big injection of cash would be helpful at the moment."

"You're not kidding it would."

"Where's Michael now?"

"He won't be back for some time," Mrs Breach said. "He's driven across to Manchester for the day, trying to sell himself to the airport."

"Has he tried the big southern airports like Gatwick and Heathrow? There must be more jobs down there."

"That's where he was at the back end of last week, over the weekend and Monday, trying to find a job."

Clare and Brett exchanged a quick glance before Clare asked, "Any luck?"

"Not a peep. It's tough without references from Sheffield – and that vindictive bitch Danielle wouldn't give him any because she's got it into her head that Mike's got a drink problem."

"I bet he's cut up about that."

"Just a bit," she said with venom.

"Is he into electronics at all?" Clare enquired. "You know, radio and that sort of thing."

Mrs Breach's brow creased.

Quickly, Clare said, "I just thought, being an air traffic controller, he'd be familiar with a lot of electrical things. That sort of expertise could give him another type of job to aim at."

Brett was impressed by his partner's quick thinking. She was trying to open up Mrs Breach by taking on the role of a chatty, sympathetic friend.

"Not really," Michael's wife said. "He says you can use a computer without knowing what happens inside, just like you can drive a car without a clue what's going on under the bonnet. But he's been known to fix a bust radio. A while ago he was more interested but not recently. I guess he overdoses on radios at work."

"That's a pity," Clare replied. "What's he qualified in?"

"Science. He's got a degree in physics."

"Did he go to school around here?"

"No. Aylesbury."

"I bet he went to a good school to end up doing science at university," Clare prompted.

Mrs Breach nodded proudly. "He's very clever. He went to an old grammar school. Why?"

"I just wondered if he got on with his old schoolmasters."

Suspicious, Mrs Breach snapped, "What's that got to do with it?"

Clare had taken her role as far as she could so she backed off. "Nothing. Just chatting. Forget it."

Brett chipped in, "Was he away looking for a job on Saturday 23rd and Sunday 24th August? Do you know?"

"The weekend before last? That was just after he was sacked. If you must know, he was round here, having the sulk he was entitled to." Without allowing the detectives to get in another question, she said, "Look, I don't like all this stuff you've started asking me. There's something going on. If you want to know anything else, come back when Mike's here. Now, the baby's going to wake up any moment and want feeding so I think you'd better go."

Brett and Clare had learned enough. Without trying to prolong the interview, they got up and Brett said, "Thanks for your help. We might take up your suggestion and call back to get a word with Michael himself some time."

Returning to their bolt-hole, Clare told Louise what they had learned about the sacked air traffic controller. While Brett entered Michael Breach's details into the folder on suspects and Clare wrote *Money?* in the Motive column, Louise said, "You're going to say you need everything I can get on Michael Breach."

"I'm afraid so," Clare replied. "We don't want you to get bored, Louise. He was educated at a grammar school in Aylesbury. His wife was my sort of age, twenty-six, so you can assume he's much the same. See if you can get hold of school reports, anyone who remembers him, that sort of thing. And he's got a car. Let's get its details, just in case it matches a vehicle seen near Kosler's action. Breach was in the London area at the time."

"That's no problem," Louise said, "but…"

"I know. You've only got one pair of hands and twenty-four hours in a day. Just fit it in as soon as you can."

"High priority," Brett added. "I make him a strong suspect – and the first we can realistically expect to get somewhere with."

It was evening. As always when she was with her parents, Clare felt a little uneasy, as if she were under test. She had bowed to pressure and agreed to drive to their house and tell them all about her trip to Tobago.

"So," her mum was saying, "you haven't even got any photos."

"It was work, Mum. I can get mug-shots of the suspects sent over, if you like."

Mrs Tilley sighed. "Well, you'd better just tell us. What was it like?"

"Sunny. Gorgeous. Laid back," Clare replied. Then she told them about the beaches, the palms, the meals, the people, the hotel.

Afterwards, her mum commented, "We hear a lot about this Brett these days, Clare. Not so much about that painter you used to go out with. What's happened to him?"

"That was ages ago. And he was in a different world. Forget him, Mum. I'm sure he's forgotten me."

"But isn't an artist a bit more … I don't know … steady and reliable than a detective?"

"*I'm* a detective, Mum. I've got a career. I'm not sure I'm cut out for steady and reliable."

"But one day you'll want to settle down with children…"

"Kids!" Clare exclaimed. "I'm not ready for house arrest yet. Besides, Brett's not that sort of partner…" He was a work colleague. That's what they'd agreed. She'd left behind any other sort of partner in Tobago.

Before Clare said any more, her dad came to her rescue. "Leave her alone, Mum. Clare'll sort it out for herself. She always knows what she's doing." He had the familiar scar down the left side of his face. To Clare, the scar had never become just another wrinkle. It was a permanent reminder of a knife attack that she had been powerless to prevent when she was thirteen years of age.

She smiled and nodded at him. But Clare wondered if he was right. For the first time, perhaps she didn't know what she was doing.

Jogging round the park early on Friday morning before the rush-hour kicked in, Brett looked up into the cloudy sky. The only large patch of blue was scarred with two parallel vapour trails of long since past aircraft. The precarious lives of the passengers were in the hands of a pilot, aviation engineers, air traffic controllers, a selfish and cold-hearted black-mailer, and the police. Brett needed to catch Strawberry before he caused a major disaster. And all for the sake of what? Revenge? Money? What was worth the life of one passenger, never mind thirty-two – or hundreds?

Why did Brett have such a feeling of dread – and excitement – when he saw the vapour trails? It wasn't as if he had any real evidence that Strawberry was going to attempt mass murder in South Yorkshire yet some inner voice told him that his involvement with the blackmailer was not going to be limited to a fleeting threat at Heathrow. No matter how much Brett told himself that he didn't trust gut feelings, he feared the worst.

At work, Louise had already passed the details of Michael Breach's car to Kosler's team in London. They would check if it appeared on any security cameras around the airports or near the drop-site for the ransom. The first three responses from inde-pendent schools had arrived. "All negative," Louise reported. "But I got somewhere with Michael Breach's school. He went to Sir Henry Floyd Grammar School in Aylesbury but it seems he wasn't … you know … the most memorable pupil. He got into the usual number of scrapes, the school said, and took maths, physics and biology at A-level. He got a respectable set of results and then went off to university. They weren't aware of any clashes with staff or other students. The science staff remember him as a bright loner."

"A bright loner," Brett repeated. "That could cover all manner of things. It certainly doesn't rule him out."

"A bright loner might be exactly what we're after," Clare added.

"I ... er ... I did a bit of other looking up," Louise said.

"And?" Brett prompted.

"Kosler's been chasing any ex-airport workers with a possible grudge – a bit like you. He's got a file set aside for them in his case notes. He hasn't got anywhere with any of them but I noticed something about one entry in there."

"Oh?"

Louise said, "I went through the Thames Valley grudge file for anyone who's got connections within fifty miles of Kinder Scout. A flight engineer called Brendan Cork was born and brought up in Broomhill. And he's living on that side of the city now – in a village called Hill Top above Dungworth."

"Interesting. Why did he come back up north?"

"He was made redundant from Gatwick."

"Have Kosler's lot looked into him?"

Louise nodded. "He claimed he was in Hill Top when Strawberry was in the London area but he couldn't prove it. They got nothing positive on him, though."

"OK. I think we want to see Brendan Cork," Brett said.

Out of Sheffield, the lane rose steeply to the aptly named hamlet of Hill Top. The flight engineer was in his front garden, pushing an old electric mower across the lawn. As the detectives approached, he cut the power, took off his flamboyant hat and scratched at his nearly bald head. He glanced at the warrant cards that Brett and Clare held out and said, "I don't know what's going on but I've already spoken to the police."

"They were inferior southern types," Brett replied, deciding to use a chatty tactic. "We're the real thing."

With an inexplicable grin, Brendan commented, "It's like being in some thriller." He seemed to be enjoying a private joke. He certainly didn't seem to be seething over his redundancy. Perhaps he was pleased to be spending more time with his roses.

Brett glanced behind him and commented, "Nice position you've got here. Great view over Sheffield."

"Yes. I'm proud of it. But you probably haven't come to sample the delights of my house." He stared at the detectives, impatient for them to get on with their business.

"We wanted to ask you about losing your job…"

"Like the others," Brendan muttered.

"Probably."

"It's an everyday event, you know," Brendan

57

remarked. "Do you send the police force out every time someone's made redundant?" He said it without a hint of humour.

"Maybe it's an everyday event but it's not nice. I imagine you're not exactly chuffed."

"You've got to be joking!" he exclaimed. "It's the best thing that's ever happened to me. The other officers asked if I had a grudge against Gatwick. No chance. It could be the other way round. Soon the airport'll have a grudge against me."

Puzzled, Brett asked, "Why do you say that?"

Brendan chuckled to himself again. "At fifty-five, I'm too young for early retirement, too old to get a proper job, so what do I do? They say everyone has a novel in them. It's true. Over the years, I've thought up a cracking plot for a thriller set in an airport. You see, I know all the ins and outs, all the weaknesses – like how you can get round Customs and airport security. I know all about intrigue among the jet set," he boasted. "I gave my idea to a literary agent and suddenly three publishers wanted to throw money at me to write it for them. I'm a novelist, rolling in money, before I reach Chapter 5. No," he concluded, "I wouldn't say I'm bitter."

Brett smiled. "Nice little earner." He glanced down at the lawnmower with its orange lead snaking across the damp grass and said, "You could even buy yourself a new mower. I haven't seen one that old for a long time."

Brendan was taken aback by Brett's shift. "There's

nothing wrong with old technology," he said, proudly defending the worn contraption.

"Can you still get parts for it?"

"Yeah. There's a shop…" He paused and said in frustration, "Why are we talking about my lawnmower?"

Brett shrugged. "I just thought I might've seen you yesterday afternoon in Electrics Unlimited. If it wasn't you, it was someone with the same sort of hat."

"I'm sure I'm not the only man who wears one."

"So it wasn't you?"

"No, it wasn't. But it is a shop I get parts from."

"Where were you the weekend before last?"

"Your southern friends only asked me about last weekend. They wouldn't tell me why, just that they were investigating some incident in the Gatwick to Heathrow area. Why are you going on about the weekend before?"

"Because we're looking into a different incident in a different place."

Cork was disappointed. "Is that all you're going to tell me?"

"Yes. That's your lot."

Brendan thought for a moment and then pointed to his house. "I was in my study, working on Chapter 3."

"What about last Monday, the first?"

"Chapter 4," he said curtly.

"Any witnesses to that?" asked Brett.

"Nothing that'll satisfy the real detectives," he

answered in a mocking tone. "My partner'll tell you I was at home but she would, wouldn't she?"

"You write straight on to a computer?"

Brendan nodded.

"So, are you hooked up to the Internet?"

"Sure. It's superb for on-line research."

"Did you go to school round here?" Clare enquired.

"I was down the hill at King Edward's – the old grammar school." Before Clare could get her follow-up question out, Brendan pre-empted it. "I had a wonderful, ancient physics master. He was like the lawnmower: a bit battered at the edges, a bit rickety, in need of some new parts, but he did a fine job. He's the one who turned me on to science."

Clare examined Brendan closely. It occurred to her that he might have a particular reason for painting a cosy picture of his relationship with his teacher. She did not detect any signs of invention but he had already admitted that he was good at fiction.

"OK. Thanks for bearing with us," Brett said. "And good luck with the novel."

Brendan gave an artificial smile, like a game-show host. He shouted after them, "You two should think about writing as well. I bet you'd come up with some great crime stories. It's got to be easier than chasing crooks."

"I'm saving it for my retirement," Brett replied, opening the car door.

Inside, Brett murmured to Clare, "If he's Strawberry, money's not the motive."

60

"I'm dubious about our budding bestseller. Too cocky by half," Clare said as she pulled away from the verge. "He says he doesn't have a grudge against his old business but the very fact that he's blowing the airport's cover in this thriller of his probably means he has."

"Maybe he works his anger out of his system quietly in his study – in his head and on paper – rather than hitting airports with a jammer."

Clare kept the car in second, using the low gear to slow the car as she drove down the twisty slope. "Maybe this novel's really his diary – recording what he's actually doing. He's Strawberry and he's writing it up as he goes along."

Brett inhaled deeply. "That's taking research to extremes but it's a great idea. I'd love to see that novel – and what happens in the next chapter."

"He might put us in it."

Brett smiled. "It's usually me that comes up with the far-fetched theories."

Clare spun the steering wheel, taking the bend where the lane became Stopes Road, and then replied, "The lowly sergeant learns from the mighty inspector."

Brett looked out of the windscreen and up at the sky. "It's closing in. Going to turn into a mucky day." Then his mobile phone rang. It was Louise. She had received a message from Danielle, requesting that they call in at the airport as soon as possible. "Tell her we're on our way," Brett replied.

Danielle explained, "After you called yesterday afternoon, I got a guy to look through surveillance tapes from the morning. And he found something that's got me worried. We had a suspicious-looking character hanging around all yesterday morning but he didn't get on a flight." She laid out some photographs on her desk. "There he is outside by the fence watching the ten o'clock arrive at ten-twenty. It's only a back view but note the hat, old pair of jeans and light shirt." She tapped another snapshot, this time taken indoors. "Here he's having a good look at the way to the departure lounge. See? It's the same clothing so it's the same man. And you've got a clear view of his face."

Brett and Clare looked at each other.

Danielle sped through more stills. "On his way to

the toilet, going back outside to watch the ten thirty take off – that's at five to eleven, having a drink in the café afterwards, leaving altogether at eleven thirty-five. If you ask me," Danielle commented, "he looks like a stereotypical actor or world-famous author: very bohemian in that hat."

"Funny you should say that," Clare replied. "We were with him half an hour ago and he's a budding writer these days."

"Really?"

Brett said, "It's Brendan Cork, retired flight engineer from Gatwick. He's got himself on a list of disgruntled airport workers."

"I see," Danielle murmured. "It's just as well I showed you these photos, then."

Brett nodded. "They don't prove anything conclusively but it means we need to turn round and go straight back to see him again."

"What should I do?"

"Nothing," Brett answered. "Leave it with us. Can we have the photos?"

"Sure. I'll get another set run off."

"OK," Brett agreed. "And keep the original tapes for us, will you? We'll pick them up later."

"I'll get Security on to it," said Danielle.

Outside Cork's house, the grass was beautifully shorn and the edges of the lawn were straight and trim. At the front door, Brendan looked surprised but not shaken. "Back so soon?" He didn't invite them in.

On the doorstep, Clare asked, "Where were you yesterday morning?"

Brendan sighed. "More tiresome questions. Why do you want to know? What's going on? Has there been another incident to investigate?"

"If you've done nothing wrong, you won't mind telling us what we want to know, will you?" Clare said.

Brendan smiled unpleasantly. "Yesterday morning, I was around here if you must know."

"Working in your study?"

"No. Working at the local airport actually."

"How do you mean?"

"I was doing research for my story."

"What's the plot of this book?" Brett put in.

"I don't know what you're getting at, but an author never discusses plots and ideas – not till it's finished and published. I don't want the starting pistol going off early."

"If necessary we can get a warrant to see the early chapters," Brett said to unsettle him.

"Look, I can tell you this," Brendan said. "It involves goods flown in to a small airport from Amsterdam. That's why I needed to take a look round at Sheffield. If you really put your Sherlock Holmes hat on, you might just be able to work out what a crook might want to smuggle from Amsterdam."

"Drugs."

There was a nasty, superior tone to Brendan's laugh. "Yes. That's what you'd guess. And that's what my readers will guess. But they're wrong. My idea's much more subtle and clever than that. But you're not going to get any more out of me, warrant or not."

Looking over his shoulder at the spectacular view, Brett remarked, "On a clear day, you must be able to see the airport from here."

"You've got better eyesight than me. That'd be nine miles away."

"Anyway," Brett said, "you've explained why you were at the airport. Did you find out all you need to know?"

"I sure did."

"So you won't need to go back." Brett wanted something to use against Cork if he reappeared at the airport in the future.

Brendan neatly side-stepped the trap. "I found out what I need for the moment – for Chapter 5. I might need to go back for more information later."

By the time that Brett and Clare picked up a sandwich for lunch on the run, cloud was settling so low that it was transforming into a fog. They drove back to the incident room with their headlights on.

So far, Louise had been informed of one ex-pupil of an independent school who'd had a personality clash with his science teacher and ended up working at a Japanese-owned computer factory in Barnsley. Louise had entered all of his details into a fresh folder. Brett decided to wait for a few more responses before following up the leads. He was also hoping that a name like Cork or Nash would emerge from the school reports. Then it would be easy to prioritize the inquiry. He asked Louise to check with King Edward VII school in case they still had records on Brendan Cork.

It came as no great surprise that Michael Breach's car had been spotted by surveillance cameras at Heathrow, Gatwick, Stansted and Luton. His job-hunting story had checked out. Mr Breach had been enquiring about ATC positions at each airport, according to the personnel managers. His car had not been picked up near the site of the failed ransom trap.

Outside, the mist gathered in the still afternoon while, inside, the small South Yorkshire team were floundering in a fog of a different sort.

Flight UK2183, an Advanced Turbo Prop carrying twenty-nine passengers from Amsterdam, began its descent towards Sheffield Airport. Expected time of arrival: 14.57.

En-route Control: "UK two-one-eight-three, you're cleared to six-zero, heading zero-four-zero. Coming up on NDB. My time to leave you. Over."

Pilot: "Affirm clearance to six thousand feet, turning zero-four-zero to non-directional beacon. Thanks."

En-route Control: "Roger. Over and out."

Pilot: "This is UK two-one-eight-three calling Sheffield Approach. Good afternoon."

Approach Control: "Sheffield Approach all ears. Good afternoon."

Pilot: "En-route ATC cleared me to six-zero, coming up on your NDB, heading zero-four-zero."

Approach: "Thanks, UK two-one-eight-three. Lock radar to Instrument Landing System. Weather when you're ready."

Pilot: "Ready. Go ahead."

Approach: "Surface wind near zero. Temperature one-nine. Caution: Code 3 landing. Thick fog down here."

Pilot: "Great! Request Flight Information Service."

Approach: "Roger. No traffic in controlled space. Overflights only. Cessna One Fifty unit last reported fifteen thousand feet, four miles east, flying VFR in upper airway, heading north. One mile west, British Airways Boeing Seven Three Seven flying twelve thousand, north to south. Unknown traffic over your shoulder, ten o'clock, five miles crossing left to right, fast moving at eighteen thousand feet."

Pilot: "Affirm. Copied information."

Approach: "UK two-one-eight-three. Descend to three thousand feet."

Pilot: "Three thousand."

Approach: "UK two-one-eight-three, turn right heading zero-seven-zero. Descend two thousand feet."

Pilot: "Two thousand. That's a roger. Right zero-seven-zero."

The airwaves lapsed into silence for a few seconds.

Pilot: "Base turn complete. Steady on new heading."

Approach: "You're not fully identified on radar, UK two-one-eight-three. Weather clutter on our screen. Resume own navigation."

Pilot: "Roger. Glide slope and direction for landing established."

Approach: "Still VFR?"

Pilot: "Negative. I say again. Negative. I can't meet Visual Flight Rules. Visibility decreasing."

Approach: "Acknowledged. I thought not. Welcome to Sheffield fog. India-Fox-Romeo."

Pilot: "Affirm IFR, Instrument Flight Rules. Flying into near zero visibility but all navigational controls OK. We're set for a hands-off landing. Autopilot locked on to Instrument Landing System and bringing us in down localizer beam."

Approach: "UK two-one-eight-three cleared for precision-monitored ILS approach to runway. Still unable to offer Surveillance Radar Approach but you're on correct glidepath and rate of descent. Looking good."

Pilot: "Passing outer marker. Twelve hundred feet. Glide slope and centreline still fully established."

There were a few more moments of radio silence. Then the pilot's tone changed.

Pilot: "Approach. I've just lost direction and altitude readings."

Approach: "What? Say again."

Pilot: "I've lost all direction and altitude readings. Navigation controls dead. I've lost GPS signals. And something's blocking the localizer beam. Complete navigation system failure. Switching to manual. I'm flying blind, Approach."

Approach: "Damn!"

Pilot: "Request urgent advice, Approach. Do I abort descent?"

Approach: "Negative, UK two-one-eight-three. I say again. That's negative. All traffic now reporting loss of navigation. We need you on the ground."

Pilot: "Copy. Coming up on runway. All clear?"

Approach: "Affirm. You're cleared for landing. Do you have visual?"

Pilot: "Negative."

Approach: "Estimate a few seconds to runway lights."

10

Brett jumped up, startled. "Say that again."

Hurriedly, Louise said, "It's a flash from Sheffield airport. The tower says they're in trouble. They've got no GPS signals."

By the time she'd finished, Brett and Clare were already at the door. "Mobilize the troops from the Operations Complex, Louise. We're off," said Brett.

"And you'd better e-mail Kosler," Clare added. With Brett, she raced down the corridor.

The pilot's first sighting of South Yorkshire land was the dual carriageway of Parkway. He breathed a sigh of relief. The landing strip was just north of the main road. He judged that he was a little low but, within the limits of his visibility, the landscape was familiar. Then he jerked upright as he saw something that he should not have seen. A line of pylons emerged one after another from the haze like the masts of becalmed ships. They should have been on his right but they were virtually scraping his undercarriage. Without GPS signals and the localizer beam, he had strayed from the flight path. The veiled runway was a hundred metres to his left. Before he could react, the aircraft jolted violently as the landing gear hit the top of a pylon and snagged the electric cables, like the rigging between masts. Sparks flew as a cable snapped and a flash enveloped the entire aeroplane. For a moment, the aircraft was a giant glowing firework, scattering embers behind it. The pilot convulsed with shock. He wasn't sure if he'd suffered a real electric shock or whether the trauma of an imminent crash had stunned him. He pulled back on the controls, desperately trying to get the nose of the plane pointed upwards. In his ear, ground control was yelling, "Climb, two-one-eight-three! Climb!"

The Turbo Prop pitched alarmingly and tilted to one side. Baggage slid and clattered across the hold, upsetting its balance. A passenger who had not secured his seat-belt flew across the cabin and smashed into the seats on the other side of the gangway. The aircraft's right wing grazed another cable or perhaps the roof of a building.

Still struggling with the controls and fighting against his own panic, the pilot steadied himself and brought the plane back to horizontal. He veered south to free the craft from the electric cables and found himself staring at the golf course on the hillside. "Climb! You must climb."

He didn't need telling. He lifted the plane's nose and watched the greens slither past, just a few metres below him. If he had left it a second longer, he would have flown into the hill.

He breathed deeply, composing himself, before being able to ask for instructions.

First, Approach asked, "What's your status, UK two-one-eight-three?"

The pilot's eye ran over his cockpit controls. In a unsteady voice, he reported, "I've got damaged landing gear and I've lost a tyre from the main wheels."

The air traffic controller swore in frustration. "Is it serviceable?"

"Unknown, Approach. Tell you when we use it."

"Have you got enough fuel to fly for fifty miles to alternative airport?"

"Negative."

"Say again."

"Negative. I'm limping. And I'm still flagged."

"Understood, UK two-one-eight-three. Instrument Landing System has failed. Maintain Visual Flight Rules if possible. Keep visual contact with the ground. Follow my directions. You need to go around and resume approach procedure. You're still cleared for landing."

"I've got one badly injured passenger, Approach, and probably twenty-eight needing treatment."

"All emergency vehicles scrambled. They're in place on standby."

"In case I bring this one down in one piece, you'd better have a stiff drink on standby as well."

"Roger, UK two–one–eight–three. I'm a bit busy at the moment but I'll see what I can do."

The officers pouring out of the Operations Complex heard the strange drone of a turbo prop labouring on an unfamiliar route, somewhere in the mist, as it circled the airport. Unusually, the place was throbbing with life. Through the haze, diffuse red and orange lights flashed from a variety of vehicles parked at the end of the runway. There was a row of ambulances to the left and fire engines to the right.

Once the police officers had dispersed into the fog, an uncanny calm descended on Sheffield City Airport. The sick whine of the aeroplane's engines was just a murmur now. Only the runway spotlights and flashing beams on the emergency vehicles remained and, at a short distance, even they were consumed by the mist.

The world seemed to be holding its breath, waiting for the next attempt at landing the Amsterdam flight. Danielle gazed out of her office window, almost paralyzed with worry, with a mobile phone glued to her ear. In the tower that resembled an outsize telephone box, Approach Control sat at his computer and talked calmly to the pilot. If he had not been concentrating so hard on doing his job under extraordinary circumstances, he might have flipped completely. The pressure kept him focused and composed. The passengers waiting for the flight back to Amsterdam had been moved out of the departure lounge that faced the runway. They crowded into the café area, where a concrete wall separated them from the incoming aircraft. They were out of the danger zone. Outside the airport premises, people due to meet friends, relatives and colleagues coming in from Holland stood by the wire fence. They were petrified, bewildered and silent. Some chewed their fingers, a handkerchief or gum. Others gripped the wire with white knuckles. A couple held each other, unable to bear the suspense. In the ambulances and fire engines, staff screwed up their faces and peered into the dense haze for the first sign of the approaching aeroplane.

And there it was. Its vague outline appeared like a ghost at the far end of the tarmac strip, floating several metres above the ground. This time, it was adrift of the centreline by only about ten metres. It veered sharply like a cumbersome truck swaying suddenly and dangerously into the right-hand lane on a motorway. Lined up with the landing lights, the metal monster dropped inelegantly on to the runway. Clouds of blue smoke sprang up from its tyres momentarily and then it bounced up into the air again. A second later, it was back down, squealing and lurching, more smoke pouring from its undercarriage. Two tyres stripped from its wheels and the plane staggered to the left.

All of the onlookers gasped. The fire engines started their engines and readied their hoses.

Then the weakened landing gear failed altogether. One of the struts buckled and the wounded plane belly-flopped on to the runway. The friction of metal on tarmac generated another flurry of sparks, threatening to set fire to any spilled fuel. The aircraft screamed like a tortured animal, skewed sideways, demolished two spotlights beside the landing strip and skidded on to the grass. Immediately, the fire-works ceased but the stricken plane careered on like a fallen skater on ice. Momentum carried it bumping over the turf. The lighted cockpit was a terrified helpless face pushing aside the stagnant fog. It was over in a matter of seconds but it seemed like hours. Gradually, the silvery creature slowed. Groaning and creaking, it came to a halt and lay on the ground like a pitiful beached whale.

The lamed aeroplane was surrounded by fire engines which immediately began to spray white foam over the wings and part of the fuselage. The escape hatch sprang open and an inflatable chute un-curled itself like a giant tongue lolling to the ground. Stressed and exhausted passengers were fed on to the emergency chute by cabin staff and evacuated from the crippled craft. Behind them, much of the plane was covered in fire-fighting froth. In a different situation, it would have looked comical.

In the car park, Clare's tyres screeched to a stop.

With Brett, she leapt from the unmarked car. Showing her ID to an airport official, Clare said hurriedly, "Is everyone down OK?"

"Just."

"Any casualties?"

"It could've been worse. I'm getting reports of broken bones and one likely heart-attack. Excuse me. I've got things to do." He dashed towards the line of ambulances waiting outside the terminal to ferry the wounded to hospital.

Brett said, "We're only getting in the way here. Let's go to Operations and see what's happening."

They jumped back into their car and sped away from the chaos. In the police building just along the road from the terminal, the pessimistic commander told them, "I've saturated the ground with as many troops as we've got but in this fog, it's hopeless. Your Strawberry could go straight past one of my officers and we'd still miss him. Without GPS, we can't get the helicopter on the job. It's too dangerous up there and visibility's negligible anyway. On top of that, we're looking at an impossibly wide area. He could be near the airport perimeter, in the park or golf course, the cemetery, the woods, in any one of the houses. He could be in a parked car somewhere. He'd hear or see the plane from any one of a huge number of places. I don't think we stand a chance of grabbing him."

Brett nodded. "I appreciate it's tricky but the alternative's giving him a free run. When reporters ask what we did to try and catch him, are you going to tell them we gave up?"

"Yeah, I know," he replied. "That's why we're doing what we can. I've deployed every last man, woman and novice. They're patrolling strategic places and I've got security cameras recording at key spots."

"What's the haul so far?"

The commander smiled for the first time. "A young courting couple in one of the bunkers and a lot of car registrations on video from surrounding roads – mainly Parkway, of course. We've stopped a few people and searched their bags but not found anything suspicious yet."

"Has the tower told you if GPS is back on line?"

"I checked. The jammer was on for almost exactly five minutes." He looked at his watch. "It was turned off thirteen minutes ago."

"So, Strawberry could have packed his bags and got out of here at least ten minutes ago."

"That's right."

"Thanks," Brett replied. "We'll take all the information from you when you've gathered it in." He turned to Clare and said, "It's under control here but I reckon they could use a couple more people on the ground."

The enormity of the task hit them as they went back outside into the overcast afternoon. Clare asked, "Where do we go?"

Brett shrugged. "No idea. Just cruise around in the car, I guess."

Of course, it was futile. With the windows down,

they stared into the white clouds and saw nothing out of the ordinary: just shadowy innocent people, buildings, trees and vehicles. Brett called Michael Breach's number and discovered from his wife that he was not at home. Mrs Breach refused to say any more about her husband and his whereabouts. Brendan Cork answered his telephone, proving that he was home in Hill Top.

"He couldn't have got there in fifteen minutes from here," Clare said. "It's right across Sheffield. Nothing gets through the city that fast."

"It's certainly tight," Brett replied.

"Admit it, Brett. It's an alibi if you still reckon Strawberry's going to be within spitting distance of the airport when he jams it."

"Mmm." For a few seconds, Brett was silent, looking out of the open window absently. Then he turned to Clare and said, "I've just had a horrible thought."

"What's that?"

"Air-band radio!" Suddenly downcast, he explained, "Strawberry's perfectly capable of making or buying an air-band radio. Aviation buffs use them to listen in to local air waves, including everything pilots and air traffic controllers say to each other." Brett shook his head. "I'm sure he could tune in to their communications from miles away."

"Like, from Hill Top?"

"I guess so. And what they say would tell him exactly when a plane was coming in to land."

Clare sighed. "Damn."

On Friday night, Brett and Clare turned up at Tim Darke's house in Hathersage. The lecturer was surprised but unruffled. When Brett asked him if he could spare a few minutes to give them some more advice, he stood to one side and said, "Sure. Come in." In the living room, he asked, "Do you want a beer?" He stopped himself and, before they could accept his offer, he said, "No. Of course, you don't drink on duty, do you? How about a coffee?"

Brett smiled. "A coffee would be good. Thanks."

Brett and Clare settled in the two easy chairs and Tim sprawled on the sofa. "We're hoping you'll be able to tell us all about air-band radios."

Tim's eyebrows rose and he glanced at his watch. "How long have you got?"

"OK," Brett said. "Let's get specific. We want to

know if they're used to pick up local airport communications and, if so, how easy it is."

"It's very easy," Dr Darke replied. "Lots of people do it."

"Why?" asked Clare.

Tim shrugged. "Beats me. But they say it's fascinating to listen to all aeronautical transmissions, especially ATC and pilot conversations."

"Some people lead very exciting lives," she responded.

Tim chuckled. He seemed to be in tune with Clare. "All they need is a VHS air-band receiver or scanner – that's about ten pounds' worth of gear up to about a thousand for the posh stuff. Add a decent aerial and Sheffield City Airport's frequency, and they can listen all day long. Most sets are simple and cheap. They're not hard to make and a lot of the big electrical stores sell them. It's illegal to use them, of course, mainly because people can tune in to police and military frequencies and monitor their communications. And they can intercept mobile phone conversations. But it's a popular hobby and the law takes a lenient view." He looked from Brett to Clare and added, "I guess you've got more important things to do. These people don't do any harm by tuning in to civil air bands."

"Who would know Sheffield City Airport's frequency?"

"Anyone with patience or a decent scanner and a bit of time. Scanners have an automatic search facility. It's like tuning into any radio station. You use trial and error or scan mode to find different broadcasts one after the other. Eventually a radio enthusiast will hit on the right channel for the airport. Either that or they have insider knowledge from the airport itself or they've got a radio navigation chart. There are several of them. They list all aeronautical frequencies and they're not hard to come by. They're even published. I dare say the information's on the Internet if you want to look. I haven't."

"So, if someone was a few miles from an airport and had one of these radios, they'd be able to pick up pilot to ground communications?" Brett enquired.

"Correct. But it's not quite as straightforward as you think. You see, the transmissions are mostly on VHF – that's basically a line–of–sight system. I'll tell you what I mean. A VHF signal travels in a straight line from its point of origin. If a receiver's directly in front of an incoming plane, it'll pick up what the pilot says to ATC. It won't be able to receive the controller's responses. To get those, the receiver would have to be in a straight line the other way – behind the aircraft. And obstructions, like tall buildings, will weaken the signal and could block it altogether. If you tried it here or on the university campus, for example, you'd be out of luck. Neither's in line with the airport runway and there'd be too much building clutter."

To get it clear in her head, Clare said, "Basically, what you're saying is, people with these air-band radios can hear either the pilot or the air traffic controller if they're in line with the runway and there isn't a tower block in the way?"

"Exactly."

"So, they'd know when a plane was approaching the airport."

"Certainly."

Brett asked, "How close to the airport would the radio have to be to pick up the transmissions?"

Tim let out a long breath. "It depends, mainly on the position and quality of the radio and its aerial, along with the number of obstacles. With a good set-up and a clear line-of-sight, tuning in from forty miles is no problem."

"Forty miles," Brett repeated, looking at Clare. "That's a long way."

"That's a headache," she responded.

"Anyway," Brett said to Tim. "Thanks for the coffee – and the information."

"Pleasure," Tim replied, taking their mugs from them.

Back outside, the fog had become a mere mist. A faint breeze had dispersed the worst of it. Brett looked up and remarked wryly, "The moon and stars in Tobago, cloud and orange streetlights here."

"No sunburn, though." Then Clare said, "Aren't we off duty now? The pub and restaurant in Hathersage does fish and real ale you'd die for."

"Yeah. Why not? One of my favourite pastimes is watching you tuck into poor, defenceless dead fish."

"Beats listening to airport broadcasts for a hobby."

"That reminds me, though," Brett said. "I want to go back into work afterwards – to consult a map."

"Yeah. I know what's on your mind. But beer and fish first," Clare replied. "Or veg curry for you."

"And I suppose you want me to have a half and do the driving."

Cheekily, she said, "I think you're getting the hang of teamwork."

In the quiet police station, Brett shifted the chairs out of the incident room so that he could spread out two overlapping OS maps on the floor. He placed a long ruler exactly on the runway of Sheffield airport. "The plane would come in to land over junction 32 and Parkway." His forefinger followed the edge of the ruler, tracing the flight path. But he swept past the airport, across Sheffield and out the other side of the city. Then he smiled and tapped the map where the contour lines congregated. "There you are." The tiny village of Hill Top was directly in line with incoming planes. "Cork's place has got a direct line of sight to the airport. Absolutely spot on. Straight and unobstructed."

Clare voiced the obvious conclusion. "If he's got an air-band radio, he could tune in to the right frequency and wait for a pilot to announce he's coming up on the airport. Easy."

Brett nodded despondently as he folded up the maps. "No need to be anywhere near it."

* * *

In the morning, Brett perched his powerful frame on the table in the incident room. He said, "I think we're all going to have to fit our Saturday shopping in some other time. Right now, there's lots of important stuff coming in – and a new issue altogether. Let's deal with it straightaway. It applies particularly to you, Louise. You see, Strawberry may well have an air-band scanner. That means he can listen to airport comings and goings *and* he can tune in to our radio frequencies. We have it on good authority that he can even intercept mobile phone conversations so, from now on, it's got to be radio silence," Brett insisted. "And we've got to be very careful about what we say to each other by mobile phone. We've got to assume he might be listening to us. I know that's going to make things awkward but I don't see we have much choice if we ever want to take this man by surprise. All right, Louise? This is mainly about you talking to us when we're out on the job."

After her mistake with a mobile phone in the Chapman kidnap case, Louise was not going to repeat the performance. She nodded. "OK. I'll remember to watch what I say."

Brett turned to the wall chart and updated it. In the *Other* column, he put *Has air-band radio tuned to airport? Also tuned to police frequency and mobile phones? BEWARE. Radio silence. Care with mobile phone communication.* Under *Location*, he wrote *Within 50 miles of Sheffield airport, Friday 5th Sept, 3 pm.*

"Is the computer system secure?" Brett asked Louise. "He could be an expert hacker as well. That'd really kill us off if he could see all our lines of inquiry and how close we are to him – or how far away."

"It's as secure as any we've got. And it'll warn me if there's an attempt to hack in."

"Right. What else? What about the casualties?"

Clare had already checked with the airport authorities. "All OK," she reported. "Four are still in hospital: three with multiple broken bones and the one who collapsed. It wasn't a heart-attack, though. Acute shock. He'll be all right."

"Thank goodness for that," Louise murmured to herself.

"Yes," Brett put in. "Twenty-nine lucky passengers and it means we're not a murder investigation. Not yet anyway."

Louise nodded. She hadn't thought of the incident as attempted murder but that's exactly what it was. Louise told Brett and Clare, "King Edward's School didn't have anything on an old boy from forty years ago. In fact," she admitted, "they said, 'You've got to be joking!'"

"Worth trying," Clare replied.

"I've been sent a huge document from the Operations Complex," Louise reported. "They've been working on it through the night and it's got the registration number of every car filmed by security cameras near the airport yesterday afternoon."

"Get them all translated into owners' names," Brett said. "That won't take long on-line to the Police National Computer. Then cross-reference the names with all the other names we're coming up with. That's suspects, any disgruntled ex-pupils in the electronics game, and our experts. Oh, and let's add a list of employees at all airports. We need to see if one name jumps out at us."

"I'll tell you one that will," Louise said.

Brett was surprised. "Oh?"

"I checked the numbers already for one particular car. One's Michael Breach's. He was on Parkway, heading into Sheffield just after the plane crash."

"Good work," Brett replied. "Thanks."

Next to him, the phone rang. Brett picked it up and said: "Lawless."

It was the commander at the Operations Complex. Brett felt free to talk openly because the call was on a conventional land-based telephone so it could not be intercepted by an air-band scanner. "Some good news and some bad," Brett's colleague announced. "We've just got a still from one of the cameras on Parkway. It's a bit blurry with the fog but it's OK. It shows someone – we think it's a man – emerging from Bowden Housteads Wood, just down the road from the airport."

"So?"

"It was taken just a few minutes after the jamming signal stopped."

"OK, but that's not exactly conclusive, is it? Could

he hear an approaching plane from there?" Brett asked.

"Absolutely."

"There must be something else that makes you think it's Strawberry."

"How often do you see someone with a briefcase taking a stroll in a wood?"

More interested, Brett remarked, "Not very. It's not going to convict anyone but push it through to my computer here, will you? What does he look like?"

"That's the bad news. We haven't got a clue. It's a shot from the waist down, I'm afraid. You've got jeans, case and a glimpse of a hand. That's all."

Brett sighed with disappointment. "OK. It's better than nothing. Wire a copy through to Greta in Forensics as well, please. Let's see what she can do with it."

When he put the phone down, the door opened and Dennis Kosler swaggered into the room. Looking round Brett's cubby-hole, the detective superintendent turned up his nose. "Call this an incident room?"

"Size doesn't matter," Brett replied immediately. "It's what you do with it that counts."

Before she had to pull the two men apart, Clare put in, "And our chief'll move us into something bigger now we know we're close to Strawberry."

"Good. Because I'll need more room for my team, see?" Kosler retorted.

12

Brett had no objection at all to sharing his information with Kosler but he was annoyed to have the man turn up on his doorstep, pull rank and take over. After all, Kosler was tarnished by his failure to trap Strawberry at the drop-site. In Brett's eyes, the Thames Valley squad had been outwitted and, to an extent, discredited. It was Big John who found the middle way. "Clearly, you remain in charge of the overall investigation," he said to Detective Superintendent Dennis Kosler, "but I want DI Lawless here to lead the local effort."

"If you want the extra pairs of hands I can..."

John interrupted the Thames Valley officer. "Anyone operating on my patch does it on my terms, Detective Superintendent, no matter how desperate I am for staff. The extortion case began down on your territory – it's your baby. But the casualties in this attempted murder came down in South Yorkshire. That makes it my prerogative and my inquiry. I'm putting Brett in charge of it. End of argument. All right?"

Dennis muttered something that passed for his begrudging consent.

Brett nodded. It was a compromise. It was likely to lead to some conflict but it was better than being shunted on to the sidelines altogether. "Yes," he agreed.

With a smile, John said, "And I'm appointing Sergeant Tilley to the serious role of keeping the peace between you."

In Forensics, Greta was scrutinizing a hardcopy of the photograph with a magnifying glass. "It's a good shot of the briefcase and jeans but I can't find makers' tags on either."

"Pity. Can we use it in some other way, Greta?" Brett asked.

"Let's blow up some bits and see," she said, shifting to the computer.

Starting at the bottom of the black-and-white photograph, Greta could not get a fix at all on the footwear and the socks remained hidden. The denim trousers were dark in colour and there did not seem to be any distinguishing features like patches or visible labels. Enhancing the image near the right hand that held the briefcase, Greta commented, "I don't think there are any rings on the fingers but I've had to enlarge it so much, it's very poor quality. It's hard to tell." She looked closely and added, "White knuckles maybe, certainly a tight grip. Whatever's in the case, it's pretty heavy." The person's left hand was hidden behind the jeans.

"What about the briefcase itself?"

"It's one of those hard ones with square corners, not the floppy type," Greta said.

"Like an executive attaché case."

"Yeah. Quite big, though."

In the crude picture, the briefcase looked black. Greta highlighted the area around the one visible clasp and the computer magnified it to fill the screen. "Ah, it's got a combination lock," she noted, tapping the screen. "It looks like a three-number combination, but it's hardly worthwhile evidence. That sort of lock's common enough."

"Better than nothing," Brett replied, standing upright again. "You carry on scanning. If you see anything else, get on to us straightaway, will you? And by that, I mean me, Clare or Louise Jenson. No one else, and not by mobile phone. OK?"

"Sure. It's your show."

"Thanks, Greta."

While Louise briefed Kosler and the Thames Valley officer went through their case notes, Brett and Clare visited Michael Breach. As they expected, he was in his late-twenties. He had close-cropped dark hair, sunken eyes, a stubbly neck and chin, and a large frame. He was both craggy and handsome. He was also perfectly sober and well spoken. He did not have the characteristic smell of an alcoholic. He didn't even have the smell of mints, meant to cover the telltale signs. Perhaps Danielle had exaggerated his problem. Or maybe she believed that the ATC job was so demanding that only a saint could carry it off.

"What were you doing on Parkway yesterday afternoon?" Clare asked, getting straight to the point.

"Is this to do with the airport? When I went past it, there was all sorts going on. Ambulances and police cars were all over the place. Then there's the news this morning. There was some sort of crash."

"Yes, but what were you doing there?" Clare repeated.

"I was on my way home."

"Where had you been?"

Michael was puzzled. "How did you know I was there?"

"You can't do anything these days without appearing on film. Your car flashed past a speed camera on Parkway."

"I wasn't going that fast," Michael began his defence.

Clare cut in, saying, "Your speed's the least of your worries. I need to know where you'd been."

Michael was distracted for a moment by the crying of his baby in the next room. The noise was not yet a panic-stricken, ear-splitting scream. Mrs Breach stood up and shuffled wearily out of the room to comfort the wakeful baby. Michael watched his wife close the door and appeared to be about to say something else to the detectives but changed his mind and answered the question. "I went to East Midlands Airport. I'm hoping they'll invite me for an interview now I've made myself known to them. Anyway, I came back up the M1, to junction 33 and along Parkway."

"Not junction 29 and through Chesterfield? It's shorter and quicker to this side of the city."

"I ... er ... heard there were road-works at Chesterfield."

Of course, Clare thought to herself, that way wouldn't take him close to Sheffield City Airport and he would never be lined up with the runway and incoming flights. "Did you stop near the airport?"

"No. I just wanted to get home."

"You didn't even linger for five minutes?" she asked as she looked closely into his face.

"No. What's this about?"

"That accident might have been sabotage…"

"And you think I've got enough of a grudge against them," he exclaimed.

"Can you persuade us that you haven't?"

"Of course I…" He stopped, calmed himself and then carried on. "Sure, I'm not happy with the treatment I got. Sure, I'm angry with Danielle. But I wouldn't get involved in any dangerous stuff. She's not worth it. When I think about it, though, I don't suppose I can prove I didn't do anything. By co-incidence, I seem to have been in the wrong place at the wrong time and, yes, I've had a disagreement with the airport. All you've got is my say-so." He looked directly at Clare and said, "Whatever happened, I didn't do it." He sighed heavily and shook his head with his eyes closed. "I suppose all the bad guys say that."

Clare ended the interview. Neither she nor Brett wanted to ask him about GPS jammers and other electronic equipment. If he was guilty, he might let slip something about blocking the GPS navigational system when they had never said that it was involved in the investigation. That would be very incriminat-ing. Besides, one day soon, they might want to get a search warrant and go over his house for electronic devices. By enquiring about a jammer now, they would prompt him to move out any damning evidence.

On the way back to the station, Clare said, "Michael Breach isn't the unreliable demon drinker that Danielle led us to believe he is. Something else is going on there, I reckon."

"Like?" Brett queried.

Clare shrugged. "No idea."

An attempted multiple murder and the imminent arrival of a big team from London did wonders for the case. The upgraded incident room had its own hot-drinks machine, plenty of wall space, more networked computers and phones. Pure luxury.

Louise had already pinned extra sheets of paper to the wall. Alongside the chart on Strawberry, there was an individual record for Michael Breach, his movements and motivations. Another gave details of Brendan Cork, the prospect of his having an air-band radio and writing the story of his GPS crimes. Yet another piece of paper was virtually blank but it was headed: *Nash*. At the bottom, Louise had written: *See computer folder for all local men called Nash (43 found)*. Then there were the details of the man – or as Louise had written it, *man?* – coming out of the wood near the airport with a briefcase. For want of a name, she had called the suspect Bowden Housteads, after the wood. She had also made out an expanding register of troublesome ex-pupils of independent schools – there were three unfamiliar names so far – and a list of expert contacts with their telephone numbers. Louise's final chart was a long print-out of car owners whose vehicles had been spotted near the airport yesterday afternoon. She had highlighted in blue the only eye-catching name: Michael Breach. Louise's appetite for work and organization was inexhaustible.

Computers were a wonderful resource. They could record and provide a vast amount of information but they also hid a lot of it. For Brett, there was nothing like being surrounded by a summary of all the data in thick felt-tip. It was an old-fashioned, permanent reminder of the bare facts. And all available at a glance. Sometimes it was the wall display that first revealed the connections, made the evidence click into place.

Kosler drew Brett out into the corridor where he could talk privately. In a discreet voice, he said, "You didn't just get the short straw with your old incident room. You got a very young and inexperienced researcher. When my men arrive, I'll replace her with a good chap called Stan."

"No chance," Brett uttered. "She may be new to the game but she's doing a brilliant job. She stays."

Dennis sighed wearily. "On your head be it, but my man'll lead the extortion angle."

"He can liaise with Louise." With a smile, Brett added, "Perhaps she can teach him a few things."

Dennis frowned. "Anyway, things'll look up when I have my own team. Let's face it, I've already got you a heavy-duty incident room."

Brett walked away back to the door. It was the changing nature of the case that had earned them better accommodation, not this irritating super-intendent, but Brett didn't want to waste time on a fruitless argument.

Dennis called after him, "At least your … what's her name? … Louise agreed to sort out hotels for me and my troops."

"She did what?" Brett exclaimed with his hand frozen on the door handle. "Forget it. She's too busy and she's not a secretary. Sorting out hotels sounds like a job for your Stan when he gets here. You don't expect her to supply coffee for your squad as well, do you?"

"Actually, yes, I…"

Brett strode back into the incident room, Dennis behind him, and announced, "Right, let's have a few local rules aired for the benefit of our visitors. Researchers do research. They don't have the time for booking hotel rooms, holidays and restaurants for senior officers. And they're far too valuable to be general dogsbodies. That's not how we operate around here. It's not about rank, it's about everyone doing their own jobs well. Louise, you take your orders from me or Clare and you use your own initiative. That's all. You don't take bullying from anyone. DS Kosler will give orders to his own officers. Now," he said, "we're off for an hour or so to work on the attempted murder. Dennis, the desk sergeant's got a list of recommended hotels in the area. I suggest you use it."

Going towards the car park, Clare remarked, "Not a marriage made in heaven, you and Kosler."

"Not exactly," Brett said. "But I was soft on him. If you were in my place, you'd probably end up battering him."

"Don't forget I'm here to keep the peace."

"Tough assignment."

On a Saturday afternoon, Electrics Unlimited was even more crowded than it had been on Thursday.

And Dylan McPhee was even less patient. Leaning on a steel cabinet with drawers labelled *Resistors* and *Fuses*, he looked at the photograph that Brett held out and stroked his chin. "Yeah," he said. "Don't ask me what he's been in to buy but, yes, I recognize him. It's the Stetson hat that gives it away."

The picture, taken by a surveillance camera at Sheffield City Airport, showed Brendan Cork. "Was he in here on Thursday afternoon?"

"I don't know for sure."

"OK. Would he have bought anything that could make a GPS jammer or an air-band radio?"

"A scanner? That's different. You didn't ask about that before," Dylan replied quickly. "But it doesn't help. I can't remember what he's been in for. All I can say is he's a regular customer."

"OK. He doesn't happen to be your Mr Nash, does he?"

"No, he's nothing like. I tell you, Mr Nash has got glasses and a moustache."

"Try to ignore them," Brett said. "*Might* he be Mr Nash?"

Dylan screwed up his eyes and took a close look at the photo. "No. This chap's too old," Dylan replied. "And, before you ask, no, Mr Nash hasn't been in since you were here last."

"You're right," Brett said. "I was going to ask. Thanks."

Outside, Clare nudged Brett and whispered, "Look." She nodded towards a young male customer who was walking away from the shop, just in front of them.

Brett nodded. It was one of Tim Darke's research students. Stefan Rzepinski was wearing the standard uniform of a Sheffield student: tired jeans and green sweatshirt decorated with the name of the last band to play a gig at the university.

Brett and Clare quickened their pace and caught up with him. "Hi," Clare said. "Stefan, isn't it?"

For a few seconds, he looked perplexed. He halted and said, "Ah, yes. You are the policemen."

The student spoke with a strong Polish accent. English was probably not his first language so Clare did not expect him to be word perfect. "That's right," she confirmed. "You've just been in Electrics Unlimited."

"Yes," he answered, his cheeks turning red.

"What did you buy?" she enquired.

"I ... er..."

"You might as well tell us," Clare said. "If you don't, we'll just go back into the shop and ask them."

He nodded. "I do not like to tell. It's ... er ... a transmitter."

"You mean a bug?" Clare moved to the edge of the pavement to let some people past.

"Yes. I believe you call it a bug," Stefan admitted.

"What do you need it for?"

"My research work."

"Wouldn't you just order it through the university if it was for work?" asked Clare.

Hesitantly, Stefan replied, "It is difficult to… Do you tell anyone else if I tell you?"

Clare shook her head. "It'll be confidential."

"After you visit, I watch Vanessa and Ken," he said in a whisper, referring to his fellow research students. "I am believing they interfere the GPS. With this," he said, tapping the pocket of his jeans, "I am hearing what they say when I am absent from the room. I know it is … how do you say? … not right."

"Underhand?"

"Yes, underhand."

Seeing Stefan touch his trouser pocket, Brett seemed distracted. While Clare carried on with the questions, her partner was lost in his own thoughts.

"What makes you think they're doing something with a GPS jammer?"

"They are using the Internet for information on the making," Stefan answered in his stilted English. "I am hoping to impress you."

"Why do you say that?"

"My career is in forensic science."

For the moment, Clare ignored his comment. "Where were they yesterday afternoon? Do you know?"

Stefan nodded. "I hear about the airplane … go bang." To make sure that they understood him, he smacked his right fist into his left palm. "Vanessa and Ken, they are not in the department. Perhaps in the library."

"Thanks for the information, Stefan," Clare replied, "but I think you'd better leave the forensic science well alone until you get the job. Leave it to the professionals." She could not take him entirely seriously. It was likely that, after she and Brett had mentioned GPS jammers within earshot of the other two students, they would be curious and take a peek at Internet sites on the topic. Even so, she knew that Brett would want to follow up the lead.

For now, they let Stefan go. Besides, it was obvious that Brett had something else on his mind. "Let's go and see Greta," he said to Clare. "I've got an idea."

"Oh?"

"Yeah. From Stefan's jeans. I'll tell you on the way."

"OK," Clare agreed. "As long as we go via Hillsborough."

"Hillsborough?"

"Wednesday against Arsenal tomorrow. I'll need a ticket. Not even Strawberry'll stop me going to that one. Are you coming? Or are you staying at HQ to make sure Kosler doesn't take over while you're away?"

Brett laughed. "I'll risk it for a couple of hours."

At Brett's request, Greta summoned to her screen the image of the unknown suspect code-named Bowden Housteads. "Yes," Brett muttered. "Let's see a close-up of his jeans, down to the knees." He paused and then said, "No, include them. Go down to just under the knees."

When the magnified picture came on to the monitor, Greta asked, "What am I doing, Brett? What are we looking at?"

"We're looking at the wear on his trousers," Brett replied. "See?" His finger traced the paths of light bands and creases across the seam of the dark fabric.

"Typical of jeans," Greta remarked. "So what?"

"Are the lines of wear typical of all jeans or just this individual pair?"

Suddenly, it clicked. Greta nodded slowly. "You

think it might be a fingerprint." With a grin, she added, "Jeans fingerprinting as opposed to genetic fingerprinting."

"Exactly," Brett said. "The question is, how unique is this particular wear pattern? If it *is* unique, we can use it to identify our mate Bowden."

Excitedly, Greta said, "Good thinking. I like it. I'll find out about wear and tear on denim. You two can help. Get everyone you know to bring their used pairs in and I'll do the same with my staff. The more, the merrier. And the more worn, the better. Then I'll have a whole range to examine. That way, I should be able to see if the pattern's always the same or whether we all wear them down in different ways, or whether one brand goes downhill in a particular way."

Brett hoped that he had found a way of getting some definite evidence at last. "We know Brendan Cork's not Bowden Housteads because he was at home when Bowden appeared on video so, for starters, you could compare Bowden's jeans with a shot of Cork's, courtesy of a surveillance camera. He was wearing jeans when he gate-crashed the airport to do his research. If this wear-pattern idea's going to get off the ground, they won't match."

Greta continued, "OK. That's a nice test but it's got to be one of many. For instance, it'd be particularly helpful to compare different makes worn by the same person. You see, as far as I know, jeans fingerprinting would be a brand new forensic method so I'd have to verify it really carefully —

especially if you're relying on it in court. If all jeans age in the same way, a match means nothing."

"I know," Brett replied. "I'll leave it in your hands then I know I'll get a good job done."

"Flatterer," Greta said. She called after him, "By the way, DI Lawless. Congratulations. It's a tantalizing idea. Clever and crafty. If you ever want a lab job, safely out of the firing line, let me know. For you, I can always find something in Forensics."

Clare sighed theatrically. "Come on, you two. Are we starting a mutual appreciation society?"

Brett and Clare asked Louise to delve into the backgrounds of Vanessa Street and Ken Price. Then, for twenty minutes, they watched Dennis Kosler briefing his displaced squad. His style involved a curious combination of rousing, encouraging and harassing. He came over as a mixture between a ruthless commander, a school prefect, a prize fighter and a school bully. When he'd finished, he introduced Brett. "Our local adviser – in charge of investigating the incident at Sheffield airport."

Brett stood up and faced the pack of hounds from Thames Valley Police. He detailed Strawberry's attack on Flight UK2183. Then he began the roll call of characters. Pointing at the wall charts, he said, "We've got a few electronics experts on our side. Dr Tim Darke at the university, his students – Stefan Rzepinski, Vanessa Street and Ken Price – and Dylan McPhee."

Before Brett could give a rapid run-down on each person, Dennis interrupted. "At this stage," he shouted out, "all the experts are suspects as well."

Brett gritted his teeth and replied, "True. But remember, there's hundreds of radio enthusiasts in the country who'd know all about jammers and any of them could make or buy one. The main local suspects are Brendan Cork, Michael Breach, mystery man Nash and the unknown walker in the wood, nicknamed Bowden Housteads." Then he talked about the evidence and definite leads so far. He ending by telling them, "I'm about to get warrants to search Breach's place and Cork's house for suspect electronic gear. I'll keep you in touch with developments. Any questions?"

From the back, a voice yelled, "Where can we get tickets for Arsenal tomorrow?"

Once the laughter had died down, Brett replied untruthfully, "It's sold out. But I'll tell you what the score was – and what a good game it was – when I get back." He hesitated before adding, "Look, in my opinion, the most useful thing you can do right now is strip off your old pairs of jeans and give them to me, Clare Tilley or Louise Jenson. We'll pass them on to Greta in Forensics."

Several men at the front twisted round, leered at Clare and Louise, and made bawdy comments to their neighbours. Brett heard one officer say, "Given a choice, I'd give 'em to Sergeant Tilley." The others seemed to agree.

"Seriously," Brett said, "we need worn jeans. You'll be doing the investigation a big favour if you volunteer any pairs as soon as you can."

Hearing a bleep from her computer, Louise got up and went to check the incoming message. After a minute, she called to Dennis Kosler, "Sir, you've got an e-mail come in from Strawberry via your people in London. They say it's untraceable."

While Dennis read the message on paper, Brett and Clare looked at it on Louise's monitor:

I hope you enjoyed my little prank. It certainly shook up a few passengers. Can you imagine it happening at Heathrow? Maybe not. The consequences of all those planes flying blind are unimaginable. To help you grasp the idea, I am going to use my jammer again. Besides, it was such fun to blow GPS away. I'm not telling you where the next lucky airport is going to be, or when it will be but you will not have long to wait. Then, even your policeman's brain should appreciate the mess you are in. Dunce's hat on, Sherlock, go and stand in the corner of the classroom. After I have embarrassed you some more, it is a million or Heathrow. Take your pick. There does not have to be a disaster. It is up to you, Kosler. As I pointed out before, if there is one, it will be your fault.

Clare noted, "Another school reference."

For a moment, Brett did not reply. He was trying to recall something. Then he quoted, "'If you put your Sherlock Holmes hat on, you'll be able to figure out what someone might smuggle from Amsterdam.' That's what Brendan Cork said to us, Clare."

Clare nodded. "It could be just coincidence. References to Sherlock Holmes aren't that unusual. We're even looking at a computer that's part of HOLMES." Information on major crimes was always stored, controlled and updated through the Home Office Large Major Enquiry System.

"True," Brett replied. "It might be misleading but both comments are used in the same way: as insults. That could be something Cork does a lot. And it's likely a writer would refer to a fictional character."

"Perhaps," Clare responded. "It's worth bearing in mind."

While Brett and Clare discussed the message quietly, behind them, Kosler was throwing orders around. Upstaged and insulted by Strawberry, he was angry. "Get on to all other airports. Get me a million in *convincing* fakes. I don't want Strawberry to be able to tell them from the real thing. Understand? Have the science boys come up with an undetectable bug yet? If not, what are they playing at?"

Brett shook his head and said, "He still thinks he can outwit Strawberry with electronic gadgets. If he tries it, he'll live to regret it."

"He's the action-man type," Clare replied. "Acts *before* he thinks. We're going to have to watch him."

The last post of the week arrived. After opening and scanning the only letter, Louise commented, "It's all happening." The letter had come from the head of science at a former grammar school in Barnsley and it mentioned a very familiar name.

Even after twenty-five years, the former pupil called Dylan McPhee was remembered for his wayward behaviour at school. Extracts from his reports showed that he was high on intelligence, low on achievement. *He has a bad attitude to school and his teachers. His extra-curricular experiments have nearly created a disaster in chemistry. If he put as much effort into working properly with electronic equipment as he does into misusing it, he would do well.* The exact reason for his expulsion from the school was not recorded but it had been something to do with the disappearance of parts from the physics laboratory. The restless young Dylan McPhee went to the local secondary school instead.

With a crooked smile Clare said, "Perhaps we've been too critical of Dennis. He did have the brilliant idea that an electronics expert might be a suspect."

"I'm glad he shared that insight with us," Brett muttered. "We'd never have managed it on our own."

Reading another message from her screen, Louise told them, "The magistrate's office can't supply search warrants till Monday morning, I'm afraid."

"Do we request another one?" Clare asked Brett. "For McPhee's house and shop?"

Brett shrugged. "I wouldn't have thought we could justify it yet. The link's too tenuous. Disruptive schooldays a quarter of a century ago don't mean his premises are likely to contain relevant evidence that will substantially aid the progress of the investigation," he said, quoting from the rule book.

"That shop of his is in Attercliffe," Louise said. "It's, you know, right in line with the airport runway."

Brett nodded. "Yeah. But it's also down in a dip with industrial buildings all round. I wonder if he could pick up airport communications from there."

Clare said, "It's got a satellite dish on one wall. I noticed it. He could have other aerials out the back. They wouldn't be out of place at an electronics shop. That would improve reception. And, let's face it, McPhee could do with the odd million."

"Couldn't we all?" Brett replied. "I'll tell you what, we'll get Kosler to put Dylan McPhee, Michael Breach and Brendan Cork under surveillance. He's probably got enough personnel."

"OK," Clare agreed. "It's a good idea in case Strawberry goes off to hit a different airport. Even if he's got an air-band radio, he'd have to be in the right place."

"True. And if Kosler makes sure they've all got a camera with them, they can take shots of the bottom half of their targets whenever they're wearing jeans. A top half shot would be useful to give us mug-shots to put up on the walls – to remind the team what the main players look like. More important, we can show them to Dylan McPhee in case any of these people are his Mr Nash. Even if Nash was wearing a disguise, McPhee might see through it."

"Good thinking. If we can persuade Kosler it's his own idea, he'll probably go along with it."

The desk sergeant installed the two callers in Interview Room 5 and then alerted DI Lawless by internal phone that he had visitors.

When Brett walked into the small room with Clare, the guests were hunched over the cassette recorder, examining it. Vanessa looked up and said, "Oh, sorry. We were just interested in your technology. It's not a normal machine."

"It's got no rewind facility so recordings can't be tampered with," Brett replied, taking the seat opposite Ken.

"I'm surprised you give the bad guys the opportunity to fiddle with the tapes," Vanessa commented.

Brett smiled. "We don't. It's so we – the police – can't tamper with the recording. We can't edit an interview after the event."

"I see," Vanessa said. "Are you going to record what we're going to say?"

"I wouldn't have thought so," Brett answered. "Unless you're going to confess to a major crime like murder."

Ken was silent, fiddling constantly with his long dark and scraggy hair, letting his fellow student do the talking.

"No," Vanessa replied. "It's nothing like that. It's just… We heard about the aeroplane up the road and put two and two together. We guessed it was a problem with GPS." She looked at her watch, "We haven't got long. We're setting up the sound system and lighting for a gig at the university tonight."

"You'd better tell us what's on your mind, then," Brett prompted.

"It's Stefan," said Vanessa. "Isn't it, Ken?"

"Yeah," the young man put in, offering his friend moral support.

"He's been behaving a bit odd since you came to our place. It's almost like he was watching us. And he's been on the Internet. We tracked what he did, didn't we, Ken?"

"Yeah."

"He's Polish, you know," Vanessa continued.

Clare broke into the conversation, saying, "That's not a serious offence, is it?"

"No, but he logged on to this weird cult-type website in Poland. We thought you ought to know because, as far as we could see, it supports terrorist attacks in the west. On one of its pages, there's a whole set of instructions on how to put together a GPS jammer. We had a good look at it and we reckon it's genuine. It'd probably work."

Clare suppressed the smile that almost came to her face. Stefan was investigating Vanessa and Ken, and they were investigating him.

Brett nodded. "Yes, I've seen this website. But thanks for letting us know. Very public-spirited of you. Were you with Stefan in the lab yesterday afternoon?"

They both shook their heads but it was Vanessa who answered. "We don't know where he was."

"Were *you* in the lab yesterday?"

"Us? No." Vanessa's responses became shorter and sharper as she realized that the detectives were interested in more than just Stefan.

Clare enquired, "Were you together yesterday afternoon?"

"Yes."

Clare guessed that they were together quite a lot of the time. "Where were you?"

"Look, we came here – public-spirited – to tell you about Stefan. We didn't expect a grilling."

This time, Clare did smile. "Believe me, if you got a real grilling, you'd know about it. I want to know where you were because then I'll know where Stefan wasn't."

Still the two students remained suspicious. Nervously, Ken pushed his glasses up on to the bridge of his nose.

"Let's be honest," Clare added. "You've just told us that you looked up how to make a jammer. There can hardly be anyone more qualified than you to put one together."

"Us and lots of others."

"Yes. Like Stefan and Tim Darke. But we're getting off the point. Where were you yesterday afternoon?"

"The library."

Clare sat back with her hands behind her head. "Yeah. That's the answer you give your boss when you're bunking off but where were you really? Come on, or tonight's band might just have to cancel."

Vanessa sighed. "Well," she began, "you probably won't believe this but it's true. You see, on Monday the university's hosting a charity quiz. There'll be a police team, we heard."

Neither Brett nor Clare reacted.

"Anyway," Vanessa continued, "we were asked to supply a few questions and set up a buzzer and scoring system, a bit like University Challenge. We were in a meeting room, working on it on our own. It's our donation to a good cause."

"That story's so fantastic, I believe every word," Clare remarked. "But why the reticence?" she asked.

"We were sworn to silence," Vanessa answered. "For one thing, Tim's on the university team and we had to keep him in the... Sorry. Nearly a terrible pun. We had to keep it quiet from him."

"How about last Saturday and Monday?" Brett chipped in. "Where were you then?"

"We had a weekend conference down at Middlesex University. North London."

"Both of you?"

The students nodded.

"And what about Stefan?"

"Yes. He came as well."

"Did you all stick together on the Monday morning?"

"No. Well, Ken and I stayed together. We did a bit of shopping and Stefan went sight-seeing."

"Have you had any dealings with Sheffield City Airport?" Clare asked. "Any connection at all?"

The two students glanced at each other. As always, it was Vanessa who answered. "No. We definitely wouldn't want to."

"Why not?"

"Well, airports aren't exactly environmentally friendly, are they? They use up fuel, destroy our green belts, and create exhaust pollution. We don't approve, do we, Ken?"

"No," he said. Ken was not the talkative type.

After the interview, Brett and Clare both agreed that the two students did not have a clear alibi. They were not at work at the time of the crash-landing and no one else could vouch for them. They needed only a quarter of an hour to get out to the airport, or to somewhere within radio range, five minutes to create havoc, and another fifteen minutes or so back to the university. They could have slotted it into an extended tea break. Also, they were in London when

Strawberry was in the same area. Yet, if they were responsible for jamming navigational signals, their motive was not obvious. Environmental protests did not usually involve a demand for money. As research students, their grants would be meagre but they were unlikely to go to such extremes to top them up. What was wrong with taking an evening job behind the bar?

Stefan Rzepinski was more of an enigma – especially if he was connected with an eastern cult. Yet he could have been surfing for jammers out of natural curiosity. It struck Brett that the three students were going round and round in circles, chasing each other's tails. Vanessa and Ken might have misinterpreted Stefan's use of the Internet, then Stefan misinterpreted their investigation, of him. But Brett had to assume that the whole episode might not have been a farce. He even had to contemplate that one of them was Strawberry, so cunning that he was making it look like farce. Yesterday afternoon, Stefan was in the Technology Department while Vanessa and Ken were away, so he must have been working on his own. That meant he was just as capable as his colleagues of slipping out and operating a jammer near the airport. Brett decided to add him to the list of suspects under surveillance.

On Sunday there was an extraordinary turn of events. It was unexpected and highly unlikely but it happened. Brett and Clare could hardly believe their eyes. Sheffield Wednesday put paid to Arsenal. And it wasn't a fluke. Wednesday deserved the win.

Returning to the incident room in exuberant mood, Clare wrote: *South Yorkshire 2, Thames Valley 0* in bold letters on one of the white boards.

Louise had left them a note. Vanessa and Ken were members of an environmental group that had protested about the building of Sheffield City Airport. They had not got criminal records but their names were known to the police because they'd been filmed at the site. They'd helped to dig tunnels and lived for a few days at the protest camp. That was before the bailiffs moved in and cleared the ground.

"Interesting," Clare said. "That gives them a grudge against airports." She pointed to the *Motive* column on Strawberry's wall chart. "That's one thing we're looking for."

Brett nodded. "We ought to take them a bit more seriously."

"But would they continue the battle after they've lost the war?"

"If they thought they could get the airport closed."

"Why threaten Heathrow and Gatwick, though?"

"Who knows? Pollution? Burning aviation fuel contributes to global warming and the ozone hole."

Clare objected, "Strawberry hasn't demanded the closure of any airport, only money."

"I said a *bit* more seriously. I'm not suggesting we put them at the top of our list of suspects."

On the way home Brett took a diversion to

Attercliffe. Just as Clare had remembered, a large satellite dish was attached high up on the side wall of Electrics Unlimited. The back yard of the closed shop was surrounded by a lofty wall but above it poked a tall spiky aerial. Brett leapt up, grabbed the top of the wall and performed a chin-up to look over. Clare's conjecture had been spot on. The aerial was fixed to the centre of the yard and a cable ran from its base into the premises. The giant antenna could have been put up to make sure of the best possible reception in the shop – for demonstrating radios before a sale – or it could have a more sinister use. Brett dropped down and dusted his hands.

On Monday morning, Brett took one search team to Michael Breach's house and Clare led another to Brendan Cork's rural hideout.

The examination of Michael Breach's place in Beauchief was futile. The most exotic piece of electronic gear was the microwave oven. It was Clare who saw the real action. At Cork's home, the officers quickly found an air-band radio. Straightaway, one of the technicians examined it and then had a quiet word with Clare.

The writer had spread himself on a couch and he was simmering. He tried to look unruffled but he was very angry. Arrogantly, he growled, "This is a disgraceful way of getting a preview of my book, Sergeant Tilley."

"Yes, I'd like to see it," Clare replied, "but that's

not my main purpose." She stood in front of Brendan and nodded towards the radio that an officer was holding. "What do you do with that?" she enquired.

"I use it to cook curries," he retorted.

Clare stared at him in silence.

"What do you think?" he said. "I listen to local airwaves. It's quite riveting, actually."

"What exactly do you tune in to?"

"Is this about the Amsterdam flight on Friday?"

"Why should you think that?" asked Clare.

Brendan smiled. "It doesn't take a genius, Sergeant Tilley," he replied. "You asked me all about my feelings towards certain airlines the other day. Now, just after a plane mysteriously drops out of the sky, you're interested in a radio that I use to listen in to airport transmissions."

"I'm told the airport's frequency is stored in your scanner's memory," Clare said.

"It would be," Cork replied. "I'm not denying that I listen in sometimes. And, yes, I know it's illegal but the police've never cracked down on such an innocuous pastime before."

"As a flight engineer, why do you think that aeroplane crashed?"

Brendan let out a breath impatiently. "I've no idea. I'd have to examine it. Listening to the local news, seeing the pictures, it seemed very odd to me. I couldn't understand it, but I understand it a bit better now you're here."

"What do you mean?"

"Given that you're asking all about it, there's an implication it was sabotaged in some way."

The team had finished their work and they had not found anything that could jam GPS signals. They had not even come across a dark attaché-type case with a combination lock. But Clare had another way of putting Cork under pressure. "You've got the local police frequency in your scanner's memory," she noted. "That's enough evidence to convict you of listening illegally to police messages. It's an arrestable offence. It's certainly enough to confiscate the radio and it's probably enough for a considerable fine. Why do you listen?"

"In a word: research."

The answer was exactly what she had anticipated but she queried it anyway. "Research?"

"For my thriller," Brendan explained in a petulant voice. "I know what's said at airports – and air-band radio helps me top up what I already know – but I also need to know *your* radio lingo. I was researching police jargon. That's all. It's perfectly innocent."

The evidence was mounting fast against Cork but it was all circumstantial. Clare decided not to arrest him for offences under the Wireless Telegraphy Acts. After all, a good lawyer would have him out of her clutches in no time. She needed something definite that she could pin on him. Instead she seized his air-band radio and a floppy disk containing the opening of his thriller on the grounds that the plot could be the same as Strawberry's.

15

In the car, Brett continued to read through the print-out of Brendan Cork's thriller. When he got to the end of chapter 2, he looked up at Clare and said, "This isn't anything about Strawberry, is it?"

"No," she replied. "Unless he slipped me a dummy story, he's not writing up his own crimes."

"Quite exciting, though. I'm hooked already. Is chapter 3 on this disk?"

Clare grinned as she shook her head. "You're not on holiday now. No time for leisure."

"It's quite good, though, isn't it?"

Less convinced, Clare said, "It's a page-turner all right." She pulled up at the airport car park and together they headed for Danielle's office.

From the window, the track of Friday's emergency landing across the grass was clear. The plane had churned up the turf, leaving a brown trail. But the aircraft itself had been removed to a hangar for study and repair.

First, Brett asked the airport manager if she'd had any aggravation from the environmental lobby. "We know you had a protest camp."

"That was before we started building."

"Yes. And you cleared it with bailiffs. But have there been any objections or threats since?"

"Nothing worthy of reporting to the police."

"Have you heard of some local environmentalists called Vanessa Street and Ken Price?"

Danielle thought about it for a moment and then shook her head. "I can't say I have."

Clare decided to change the subject and get down to the real reason for their visit. "Tell us again," she said, "why you felt you had to sack Michael Breach."

Danielle looked startled. "I thought I'd made it absolutely clear. When you have a few drinks, you don't drive a car, fly a plane, or control air traffic. It's just not done."

"Well, we've seen Michael a couple of times now and we've seen no evidence for his drink problem. I agree he might look a bit rough but he seems perfectly sober."

Danielle suggested, "Maybe he's learnt his lesson and cleaned up his act before he goes for another job."

There was something about the way Danielle crossed both her arms and her legs defensively. Clare said, "What's the real reason you wanted him out?"

Suddenly wary, Danielle asked, "What's Michael said?"

Clare decided to bluff it out. "He's told us everything – from his point of view. Now, we need to know how you see it."

"Well," Danielle began, "I don't know why you're so interested in our little … squabbles."

"It might be a little squabble to you," Clare said, "but you can never tell how someone else'll react. That's what you said before. I think you were right. So, in case a little squabble's turning into a major incident, you'd better tell us your side of the story."

With a weary sigh, Danielle replied, "All right. I'm still surprised Michael told you. I bet his wife wasn't around at the time."

Clare said, "No, she wasn't."

"I suppose it started almost as soon as he took the post here. I guess he'd claim he wasn't getting much attention at home. His wife was heavily pregnant. She had more on her mind than her husband."

To encourage Danielle, Clare gave a knowing nod.

"So, we had a bit of a fling. That's how Michael described it. A bit of a fling." She shook her head. "Obviously I took it far more seriously than he did. You may have noticed he's very attractive, in a rugged sort of way. Rough was the word you used." She paused before adding, "I bet you think I'm really bad because his wife was pregnant at the time but I didn't start it. It was Michael who came on strong first. Anyway, typical man, when his son was born, he decided he really loved his wife and off he went. He ditched me without a second thought."

"Isn't it understandable that Michael thinks you sacked him out of spite?"

Danielle leaned forward. "No, it's not. When we broke up, Michael had a good few drinks. He'll say, 'Oh, I just needed some whisky to pluck up the courage to dump Danielle,' or 'I was worried Danielle would tell my wife,' or something. But that's not the point. He didn't lose his job because he ditched me. He jeopardized my airport. That's stupid and irresponsible."

"OK," Clare said. "I think we get the general picture. *You* feel aggrieved because he chose his wife over you and, when you felt you had to sack him, he got the wrong idea. *He* feels aggrieved because he thinks he was really sacked as a punishment for breaking up with you. And he reckons you're not giving him a reference for the same reason."

"I guess that covers it," Danielle replied, "even though what he believes is nonsense."

"Right. Thanks for clearing that up. Now we can see what we're dealing with."

"Is he really so sore that he'd have a go at the airport just to get back at me?"

Standing up, Clare replied, "We don't know yet. And why would he threaten to attack Heathrow?"

Danielle did not have an answer.

In the car park, Brett turned the whole idea on its head. He asked his partner, "Do you think Danielle's so sore about being ditched that she'd sabotage her own airport just to throw the blame at Breach?"

"That's taking a little local conflict a bit far, isn't it? And I still think Strawberry's a man. Besides, why would Danielle threaten Heathrow?"

Brett shrugged.

Clare said, "Well, we'll soon find out, according to Strawberry's e-mail. If he strikes at a different airport, the idea's out the window, as far as I can see. If he attacks Sheffield again... Well, you might have a point."

As he locked his seat-belt into position, Brett said, "I'll tell you why this case is tricky. There isn't a real scene-of-the-crime in the usual sense. Strawberry doesn't have to be at the scene of his crimes at all so we've got no contact or trace evidence. I begin to hanker after a drop of blood, a bit of mud, a shoe print, anything. And, on top of that, he doesn't use a conventional weapon. There aren't any wounds to examine, firearms residues. Nothing."

Clare smiled. "All you've got for Forensics is one dodgy photo. You must feel naked."

Much to Brett's surprise, his mobile phone rang. It was Dennis Kosler. "Just to let you know," the DS said, "I'm sending my men out to check on schoolkids who clashed with science staff but went into science careers anyway. We've got quite a list now. I'm going after one called N—"

"I don't want this conversation by cellnet, Dennis. Tell me when we get back. For now, just make sure your gorillas don't beat them all up." Annoyed, Brett put the phone away and muttered, "The man's a pest. John thought Louise might be a liability but we've got ourselves a different one altogether."

As soon as they walked through the door, Louise was updating them. The name that had excited Kosler was Wayne Nash. Dennis could not wait for Brett's return. Louise had tried to tell him that using the mobile phone was not a good idea but she was not persuasive or authoritative enough.

"Let's hope Kosler asks Nash if he buys things at Electrics Unlimited. Even better, he could bring back a photo of this particular Nash so we can show it to Dylan McPhee and find out if he's the mystery customer."

"And I got in touch with Ken and Vanessa's schools," Louise said. "Ken Price got sent to a boarding school but there's no reports of clashes. Vanessa Street went through a normal comprehensive. The head teacher called her an exceptional talent. That's all."

"Oh well. Anything else?" Brett asked.

"You got a message from Detective Sergeant Yelland," Louise replied. "It's a reminder about the quiz, seven o'clock tonight."

Clare nodded, looked at her watch and said, "Let's go and freshen up. We both need to look our gorgeous best if the cameras are going to be there."

"Good luck," Louise said. "Hope you win."

*　*　*

The university room was packed with rowdy
students and staff in high spirits. Vanessa and Ken
lurked in the background in case the electrical
system needed running repairs. Unfortunately the
TV cameras had not turned up but the host and
question-master wanted to get on with it anyway. He
introduced the teams and the occasion. "The prize is
a bottle of champagne but, of course, because it's all
for charity, the winning team will be expected to put
it up for auction and get a bit more money for a really
good cause. OK," he announced, "let's have a bit of
quiet and we'll get going with the first question. A
starter for ten points. In John Carpenter's film, how
many people survived *The Thing*?"

Immediately, the Fraud Squad officer pressed the
buzzer. "Two. But one of them might have been
infected with The Thing. So, by morning … you
never know."

"Very good," the host said among the applause.
"Right, the police get three supplementary questions
on Switzerland."

Mark Yelland sat upright, taking particular note.

After twenty minutes, the Yorkshire Television
crew turned up and disrupted the proceedings. The
question-master took a short break so that the
cameras and sound could be set up. While the TV
crew reorganized the place for their own convenience,
the sound engineer apologized for their lateness.
"You see, something cropped up. There was a naked

125

man threatening to throw himself off the roof of the National Centre for Popular Music. You know, it's housed in those new buildings that look exactly like the things you play curling with – only bigger."

Someone said, "They're called curling stones."

The question-master joked, "That's ruined my next question."

"Whatever," the soundman said. "But we had to go and cover it for local news. It took a while to find the right angle to make the story decent."

By the time the quiz was drawing to a close at eight o'clock, the lawyers were out of it, lagging a long way behind. Sheffield Academicals were in front of the Cute Constables by a short neck but the police team could win it by answering the final starter and at least one of the supplementary questions. With dramatic hesitation, the host announced, "Right. It's all down to this." He waved his last card. "Ready on your buzzers." The room was absolutely quiet for the first time. "In aviation, what's a localizer beam?"

It was Clare's hand that got there first. She answered, "It's a radio signal that planes use to mark the centre of the runway when they're coming in to land."

"Absolutely bang on. That draws you level with the Academicals."

Brett was puzzled. Out of the corner of his eye, he'd noticed that Tim Darke had not made a move towards his buzzer even though he must have known the answer.

The question-master said, "You need to get one supplementary question right to take the competition outright. The topic is … tropical fish."

Clare and Mark grinned broadly and turned towards Brett.

Arms aloft theatrically, the four triumphant police officers received cheers and good-natured jeers from the crowd. With the cameras still rolling, they were presented with their champagne trophy and immediately donated it to a charity auction. While the chaotic bidding got underway, Brett's mobile phone reminded him that he was still on duty. Louise almost shouted into his ear, "The eight-fifteen landing at Sheffield's in trouble, Brett!"

Brett grabbed Clare and dashed from the stage, watched in amazement by the losing teams. Mark shrugged and explained his team-mates' odd behaviour in two words: "Police work."

As the car screeched away from the university, Brett's mind was still on the quiz. He said, "That last starter question on radar was right up Tim Darke's street. Yet he didn't answer it."

"You reckon without my lightning intelligence," Clare muttered as she swung the car violently round a traffic island. "I just beat him to it."

"It's got nothing to do with your lightning intelligence," Brett replied. "He didn't go for it at all."

"Not even university types know everything. We asked him all about jammers and scanners – and he knew about them – but we didn't say anything about localizers. Maybe we should have."

"No maybe about it." Blaming himself, Brett said, "It was a bad mistake. Anyway, I'm sure he'd know about them."

Clare frowned. "Perhaps he didn't want to appear familiar with them in front of us."

"That's what was on my mind as well," Brett said as they swung on to Parkway and Clare put her foot down, joining the hordes of cars charging along the dual carriageway like a herd of buffalo. "If he's Strawberry, he wouldn't want to show off his knowledge of localizers. But, if the jammer's going now, he's out of it. He was sitting right there when we left."

"Yes. Vanessa and Ken are off the hit list as well. Stefan wasn't there, though, as far as I could see."

"No, I didn't spot him either," said Brett.

"Boys in blue up ahead," Clare remarked.

Brett held his warrant card against the side-window while Clare overtook the squad car, well beyond the speed limit. The police constables inside would radio in Clare's registration number. In a few seconds, they'd get confirmation not to chase the speeding vehicle because it was in the hands of the CID.

When Brett and Clare ran into the airport grounds, they assumed that it was a false alarm. The Turbo Prop was standing happily on the tarmac beside the terminal and passengers were emerging uneventfully from the building. The scene was nothing like the tense episode of Friday afternoon.

Yet Danielle and the pilot confirmed it. On the final approach the GPS system died. But this time, visibility was good and the rest of the instrument landing system functioned perfectly. Even without navigational control, the airport mounted a flawless ILS approach to the runway. The aircraft's glidepath and rate of descent were fully established throughout the landing.

"I got the passengers down," the pilot told them coolly, "before they knew I was flying blind. It wasn't a problem at a small airport where there's hardly any other traffic around. At Amsterdam, with its crowded air space, it would have been a disaster. I dread to think. All those planes flying without navigation, the chances of collision would be very high, especially if it was night-time. Even with all our gadgets and fail-safes, the outcome would be very different."

The Operations Complex had mounted yet another thankless operation. And early reports suggested that it would draw another blank. When the officers were called back to base, probably empty-handed, they'd examine all security footage and forward anything of interest to Louise Jenson.

Heading towards the city on Parkway again, Clare was feeling content. "It's been a good night," she declared. "We won the quiz, the passengers got down in one piece, and we knocked three people off the suspect list – Tim Darke, Vanessa Street and Ken Price. Not a bad evening's work." In addition, she'd had an opportunity to drive fast. It could only have been better if there'd been a car chase.

Thinking aloud, Brett murmured, "Yes. We got off lightly. A bit too lightly." Then he said, "Anyway, we need to know where our suspects under surveillance were."

When Brett repeated his comment in the incident room, Dennis snapped, "I've got that information already, see? Most of it anyway. Brendan Cork was at home. That doesn't tell us anything if he's got hold of another air-band radio. He still heads my hit list. Stefan Rzepinski's on the university campus – unless he sneaked away and back again. We don't think he did but the building's got too many exits for us to cover them all. Anyway, he's still working, I assume. Monday's late opening for Electrics Unlimited. I called in myself. Dylan McPhee was at the shop until a few moments ago. Michael Breach we lost, I'm afraid. All we know is, he took off from home in his car at twenty to eight. We've got to put him down as a don't know."

"How do you know all this?" asked Brett.

Dennis gave him a withering look. "You're too sensitive about this eavesdropping on calls. Anyway, I kept radio silence. I got my men to call in from phone boxes."

While he added *Within 50 miles of Sheffield airport, Monday 8th Sept, 8.15 pm* to the *Location* column of

Strawberry's chart, Brett enquired, "What about Wayne Nash? Any joy?"

"Not a lot," Dennis reported. "He *has* used Electrics Unlimited but I got a photo of him and showed it to McPhee. He says Wayne isn't the mystery Nash. Actually, we showed him snaps of a whole number of people and he didn't recognize any of them as Nash. I think he's hung up on the moustache and glasses. We'd have to scribble them on each photo before McPhee'll come up with the goods." Kosler looked at Brett, adding, "And we haven't got anything else out of your idea of tracing troubled kids at independent schools." He made it sound like an accusation.

After Dennis had gone, Louise whispered to Brett, "Superintendent Kosler's right. He didn't use radio, you know. But he used his mobile phone once or twice. I saw him. He could've just been ordering a pizza but, if that's all it was, he didn't get one for me. And Stan called some of his team with a mobile."

Brett nodded. "You make a good spy. Keep it up."

Louise looked from Brett to Clare and said, "Well? Aren't you going to tell me?"

Clare ran a hand through her red hair and replied with a grin, "We slaughtered them. With all their degrees and PhDs, we stuffed them."

16

Strawberry was enjoying himself immensely. He was toying with them all, tying the police up in knots. He didn't need to bring down another aeroplane. His purpose was served simply by giving them another burst of a jammer. Exactly five minutes. He'd made sure that the timing was precise. It was a beautiful scheme. Even with their limited imaginations, the authorities would be able to smell the disaster-in-waiting. In their brains, they needed only to add another fog, darkness, or more aeroplanes to the equation and they would detect the coming stench of tragedy. "Not a bad evening's work," he said to himself gleefully as he drove through the deserted, lamp-lit streets of Sheffield. "And it's not quite over yet." He still had a message to deliver.

He could almost taste success. It was deliciously

spicy. Much to Strawberry's surprise, GPS was turning out to be his friend after all. He sniggered. It could stand for Getting Police Stumped! And there was another reason to feel pleased. He was up against a worthy opponent at last. Kosler had faded into the background as befitted an incompetent jerk and instead the police had given him this Lawless character who presented a more suitable challenge. It would be a real pleasure to defeat him. Strawberry laughed aloud. He had no doubt at all that he would dupe both Lawless and Kosler. Soon, even Brett Lawless would beg him to take the money.

The e-mail from Strawberry came in during the early hours of Tuesday. When Louise booted the computer in the morning, notice of its arrival was splashed across the screen. The first of his messages had been re-routed through a double-glazing company and the second through a kitchen designer. This e-mail had also followed a false trail to disguise its true origin. It appeared to have come from *The Citizen* newspaper office.

I think I have your undivided attention now. You can see that I will do exactly what I say I will do and you cannot stop me. My next port of call is somewhere within range of both Heathrow and Gatwick. For me, that is a much easier target than Sheffield. There are so many planes to aim at. On Monday 15th September I will use the jammer for a fixed period of time. However, I cannot tell you how long that period will be. I will leave it on until two aeroplanes crash. Now there's a sobering thought. It could be 1000 lives. How much are they worth? Some would say a lot but I am giving you all those lives for a mere £1,000 each. That is a small price to pay, a real bargain. You have the rest of the week to find £1,000,000 for me. I will collect it at the weekend. No tricks and no bugs. If I think you are trying anything on, I will leave it. If I don't get the money or it is tainted, you are going to have one hell of a Monday morning feeling. After that, the price will soar while the planes nosedive. It will be two million next.

How does it feel to be sidelined, Kosler? Not nice, is it? Still, you deserve it. And at least it means I get a worthwhile opponent in this Lawless chap. Not that it will make any difference to me. I will have my money whoever hands it over. I will be in touch with instructions.

Clare studied the message carefully and then said to Brett and Louise, "There's a couple of really interesting things here. *How does it feel to be sidelined…? Not nice is it?* That sounds like personal experience. My guess is, Strawberry's been overlooked for something."

"Maybe it's that school thing again," Brett suggested. "Perhaps it's his intelligence that was overlooked and that's why he feels sidelined."

"Possibly." Clare did not sound convinced.

Brett prompted, "You said a couple of things."

"Yeah," she replied. "There's something not quite right about your fan." She explained, "This memo and his last one aren't consistent. Not really. He says he likes a challenge. He prefers it now he's up against you. But he also said it was fun to blow GPS away. But that's no great challenge. We know from Tim Darke, Vanessa, Dylan McPhee. They're all telling us it's easy to jam GPS signals if you've got the right knowledge and equipment. So, where's the challenge? Why is it fun to him?"

Brett shrugged.

"Well, perhaps he's got a personal gripe to do with GPS," said Louise.

"Like what?"

"I don't know," she admitted. "I was just thinking. If there's no challenge and he still enjoys it, he must have something against it, like. That'd make him feel good about messing it up."

"That's true," Clare said. "When I was at school, it was easy to beat all my mates at swimming. Once I'd got over the show-off stage, it was no great fun. But it still felt good to beat a girl called Tara because we didn't get on. Actually, it was wonderful because she was really horrible."

"I can see that," Brett said, " but how can you have a grudge against a *thing*?"

"Easy," Clare replied.

Instinctively, Brett knew that his partner was referring to her intense dislike of knives. He didn't pursue the argument.

"Besides," Clare added, "you were happy with the idea that Strawberry might have something against an airline, so why not GPS as well?"

Brett held up his arms in surrender. "OK. You two think Strawberry doesn't get on with GPS. The question is, why not?"

"I don't know," said Clare. She turned towards Louise.

"No," Louise said, reddening. "Nor me."

Brett came to a decision. "All right. It's a bit strange, I reckon, but we'll see if we can follow it up sometime, somehow. For now, put it on the chart, Louise. It's your idea."

With a felt-tip, she wrote *Personal grudge against GPS?* in the *Motive* column.

Brett hesitated, looking at the apparent origin of Strawberry's e-mail, before saying, "Here's something. Isn't *The Citizen* owned by Dodwell Publishing?"

"Yes," Clare replied. She knew because she had a friend who was a reporter at *The Citizen*.

They were joined by Dennis Kosler who had overheard the question and answer. Immediately commandeering the conversation, Dennis grunted, "What's your point?" Clearly irate, he had obviously taken Strawberry's cutting comments to heart.

"Dodwell owns a publishing house as well," Brett said. "I remember reading about the take-over. It's amazing what people will do to pass the time on a long-haul flight: even browse those dreadful free magazines they have on planes."

Brett would have asked Louise to find out which

company was going to publish Brendan Cork's thriller but she was already fishing for information on the writer's floppy disk. "Yes," she said, "there's a letter here to his publisher. It's called Colossus Press."

"Get on to their website, Louise. Who owns them?"

Within a few minutes, Louise pointed at her monitor. "There you are." At the base of the web-page, it read, *Colossus Press is wholly owned by William Dodwell.* Strawberry's e-mail had come through a company connected with Brendan Cork.

Teasing, Clare said to Brett, "Happy now? You've got some physical evidence, not just a gut reaction to Strawberry's psyche."

"It's not—"

Interrupting Brett, Kosler jumped at the evidence coupling Strawberry's caustic e-mail with Cork's publishing house. He cried, "That's it! At last, we've got a link. At last, he's been careless." Turning to his men, he ordered, "We're on our way to Cork's place to arrest him." A contingent of the Thames Valley team was out of the door before Brett and Clare could voice their reservations.

While Kosler contemplated an early and hasty end to the case, Brett asked Louise to cross-check Friday's haul of registration numbers with the vehicles that had been in the vicinity of the airport yesterday evening when a jammer had been operated. He wanted a list of any cars that had been near by on both occasions. "Then," he said, "we get Kosler to put his troops on the task of chasing them up. At least it'll keep them out of the way and make them feel wanted."

In Interview Room 2, Kosler's sidekick rocked back in his chair, looking cool and hard. Dennis Kosler remained upright and growled at Brendan Cork, "When we came to arrest you, you were in your back garden by a pile of freshly dug earth. Why's that?"

"I'm a keen gardener," Brendan retorted. "I was wondering what the moles had been up to."

"Nothing to do with the GPS jammer that we found in the hole?"

"No."

"I'm not a fool, Mr Cork. I suggest you were burying it to conceal it till you're ready to use it again."

"No. I didn't know it was there and I certainly didn't bury it."

"Come on! How did it end up in your garden, then?"

Brendan slowed his speech deliberately to annoy the impatient detective. "That's a good question, DS Kosler."

"Meaning?"

"Meaning, I don't have the foggiest."

With a cynical sigh, Kosler said, "Are you claiming it's a plant?"

Cork's face twisted into a sneer. "Well, at least that would explain why it was in my garden."

Kosler leaned forward and stared into Cork's

bright eyes. "You're in serious trouble, you know. Heavy-duty trouble."

"I would be, if you'd got anything that proved I'd buried the treasure. Has it got my fingerprints on it? I doubt it very much."

"We'll soon find out," Kosler replied. He had sent the electronic device and its paper wrapping to the forensic department for trace analysis.

While Kosler grilled his man, Brett was considering the unusual find in the writer's garden. "I can think of three possibilities," he was saying to Clare and Louise. "First, Cork's perfectly innocent yet he has a jammer. We missed it on the search yesterday, but our arrival made Cork realize it could incriminate him if we ever did find it. As a flight engineer, he must know that a navigational problem could've caused the accident on Friday. So, he tried to hide his jammer by wrapping it up and sticking it down a hole. Marks out of ten, everybody?"

"Zero," Clare replied immediately.

"Louise?"

"I don't know. But it sounds unlikely. Why would he have a jammer thing if he's, you know, on the level?"

"Right," Brett said. "We'll call theory one highly improbable. Second theory. He's guilty. He was hiding his jammer for a few days before his Heathrow strike. What do you think?"

"I hate to go along with someone like Kosler,"

Clare put in, "but, let's face it, everything points to Cork. He's up there among our best bets."

"Agreed. He'll say the jammer was planted on him, though," Brett guessed. "That's probably what he's doing right now. Anyway, the third theory says he's innocent and someone's trying to dump him in it."

"Another zero out of ten if no one on the outside knows he's a suspect," Clare said.

"True," Brett agreed. "But what if someone *does* know he's a hot suspect?"

"It means our security's up the chute."

"Exactly."

They both looked at Louise, not because they were accusing her of leaking information, but because they thought she might be able to shed some light on it.

She stammered, "I don't think it was me. I hope it wasn't. I didn't … you know."

"Don't panic, Louise. We trust you. Were there any attempts to hack into the computer?"

"No. None recorded."

At that moment, a hassled Kosler walked into the incident room. Brett and Clare looked at each other knowingly. Instead of asking Dennis about the interview, Brett said, "Have you or your men been in contact by radio or mobile phone?"

"No," Kosler claimed. "Well, not a lot. It's hard to co-ordinate things without communication, see?"

"Have you mentioned Cork's name on a mobile?"

Kosler shrugged. "Possibly, but I still think you're exaggerating the problem of Strawberry listening in."

Clare sighed loudly and Brett threw up his hands. "But if he was eavesdropping, he'd know we were on Brendan Cork's tail. Hacking into Cork's computer would tell him which publisher's bought the thriller. I'd say it'd be pretty easy to stitch Cork up."

Clare added, "Strawberry would think it was great fun to plant some evidence on someone else."

Irritated, Brett concluded, "I'll leave it to you, Dennis, to tell John Macfarlane why we're releasing Brendan Cork without charge."

"Release him? You can't be serious! Cork's our man."

"Yeah, he might be," Brett retorted. "But we won't have a case against him now."

Dennis argued, "We just need to work on him a bit more."

"You can put him on a rack if you like," Brett responded, "but you won't get anywhere – even if he's guilty. You've broken our security. Let him go before a lawyer forces you into it."

"We might be letting Strawberry walk free – after he's threatened to kill a thousand people."

"I know. Keep him under surveillance," Brett suggested. "We can grab him again if we get some real evidence linking him with the jammer – like a strand of his hair in it. That's about our only option now."

G reta was swimming in a sea of jeans, photo–
graphs of jeans, and the output from pattern
recognition software. She was just keeping her head
above water. "Thinking of opening a clothes shop?"
said Clare.

"No," she replied. "I'm sick of the sight of jeans."

"But are you getting anywhere?" Brett enquired.

"Just call me a jeans genius."

Straightaway Brett's dark mood, brought on by
Kosler, began to lift. "Oh?"

"I need to do more basic tests but there's a good
chance you've come up with something, Brett. It's
even been used before. Only once and not in this
country, though." Greta told them, "Earlier this year
in the States, a surveillance picture of a bank robber's
jeans got him convicted because of the unique wear

pattern. His ancient jeans matched it exactly. Pity it was in America but, even so, it's a precedent."

"What about your own research?"

"The wear pattern follows slight imperfections when the trousers were made. I consulted a materials expert and a used-jeans exporter. They reckon there's a whole range of factors – like the shape, posture and behaviour of the body underneath – but they both agreed the wear depends mainly on the way the denim gets pushed through a sewing machine to do the seams. You see, it's not automated. Every factory worker does it differently on each pair so the fabric gets stretched and bunched up unevenly. Then, any slightly raised bits are worn away quicker, giving those white lines on all our jeans – and on the photo."

"That's good news."

"No," Greta replied. "It's brilliant news. Every pair of jeans has got a unique fingerprint of wear." She shuffled the dozens of photographs and commented, "Pattern recognition software can distinguish every one of these. I've done blind and double-blind runs, and it hits the target every time."

"This is all too good," Brett replied. "What's the bad news?"

"There isn't any really," Greta said. "Statistically, I still need to examine fifty more pairs before you'll put me in court to swear it works. It's an on-going item. And I suppose it's a pity Bowden Housteads didn't have patches on his trousers as well. That would've made them even more distinctive. Even so, we've got a denim fingerprint. All you've got to do is find the trousers that match the wear pattern."

Clare murmured, "Maybe *that's* the bad news."

"Anyway, it's a great piece of work, Greta. Thanks," Brett said. "How about the GPS jammer one of Kosler's people brought down?"

Greta shook her head. "I've got a scientific officer working on it right now for prints and traces. I'll let you know if he comes up trumps."

"Is it a commercial product or a home-made device, though?"

Greta replied, "It looks home-made to me but I've got a specialist coming over to make sure. He'll compare the circuits with those website instructions and see if there's a match. Then we'll be able to tell you where the design came from."

Brett nodded. "Yeah. That'll be helpful. So would a list of components. I'll be able to find out if they could've come from Electrics Unlimited."

"I'll get him to e-mail a list as soon as he can."

"Thanks. How's it powered, by the way?"

"It takes a battery but it's got a socket so it can be run from the mains as well," Greta said.

"What about the paper it was wrapped in?"

"It's common brown stuff, available at any retailers. There's no lead there, I'm afraid. I've got someone going over it but it won't do any good because it's too contaminated with soil. We'll be able to tell you quite a lot about the garden it was buried in, but not much else."

On the way back to the incident room, Clare said, "Of course, there's no guarantee Bowden Housteads is Strawberry. And if he isn't, all this jean finger-printing is a waste of time."

"True," Brett admitted. "But there's a reasonable chance he *is* Strawberry. Anyway, I'd like to hear an explanation of what Bowden was doing in the wood near the airport with a heavy briefcase."

The low cloud that blurred the hills drifted down lightly into the city. It didn't rain, wasn't exactly foggy, wasn't exactly fine. It certainly wasn't summer and it wasn't properly autumn. It was just a typical damp and misty September day in Sheffield. The leaves on the trees were just beginning to turn. Not fully green, soon they would be red, yellow and brown. Then they would be ripped forcibly from their wooden moorings by the first vicious wind of autumn to litter the parks and streets. If it rained they'd form a soggy, slippery mulch. If it was dry they'd become as brittle and crunchy as eggshells.

In his university office, Tim Darke smiled and got to his feet. "Welcome." He held out his hand. "I didn't have time to congratulate you last night. You put up a good performance." He took particular pleasure in complimenting Clare. "Last time I saw you, you were fleeing from the scene of your victory."

Not giving much away, Clare commented, "Always on duty."

Tim sat down again and waved the detectives

towards a couple of seats. "What can I do for you?"

Getting straight to the point, Clare asked, "Do you think anyone would bear a grudge against GPS?"

Tim looked puzzled. "How do you mean? You can bear a grudge against a person but how can anyone bear a grudge against a navigational system?"

"Can you think why someone might?"

Tim shrugged helplessly. "In a word, no."

"Who developed GPS?" Brett enquired.

"The Americans, of course, and the military in particular. They needed it to orient their guided missiles. Anyway, they put the first satellite up in orbit in 1978. Now, there are twenty-one and a few spares in case of failure."

"When did it get used for civil aviation, then?"

Tim twisted round on his mobile chair and crossed his legs, revealing another pair of odd socks. "Well, it was offered in the early eighties but the authorities took a long while to be convinced it was reliable. Once they accepted it, it was phased in throughout the nineties. Now, someone's decided to make it the sole navigation aid, withdrawing ground-based nav-aids, except for the few they'll keep to monitor the accuracy of the satellite system."

"Is there a problem with that?"

"Some say so. It's the problem you know well," Tim replied. "GPS signals are easily jammed by accident or on purpose."

"Is there a rival system?"

"GLONASS. The Global Orbiting Navigation

Satellite System, developed in Russia and Poland."

"Poland."

"Yes. It's still a satellite-based nav-aid. It's being combined with GPS for world-wide coverage."

"How about a better system that's not prone to jamming? Is there one?" Brett queried.

"Not in operation. You could've updated the network of ground-based beacons, I guess. But not now. They're being phased out. The authorities are replacing them with the hi-tech option: GPS and GLONASS. They've thrown such a lot of money and resources at satellites, they can't abandon GPS now. They're going down a one-way street."

"Interesting," Brett murmured. Then, recalling a previous oversight, he asked, "How easy is it to knock out an airport localizer beam?"

"You mean, in a power cut? Not easy at all. It'll have a back-up generator."

"No, I mean, how easy is it to interfere with it electronically so a plane can't sense it?"

Tim drew in air noisily between his teeth. "I've never really thought about it. But I guess it's like any other radiofrequency beam. You could confuse a plane by sweeping the whole area with noise on the same frequency. Then the pilot's landing system won't be able to lock on to the localizer." Concerned, Tim looked at them and said, "It'd cause pandemonium, that I do know."

Ignoring Tim's anxious expression, Brett checked, "So, it'd need another transmitter?"

Tim nodded. "Correct. And quite a heavy power source, I'd say."

"One that would fit into a briefcase?"

"Quite possibly."

"Talking of localizers, I couldn't help noticing you didn't answer the question on them last night," Brett remarked.

"No, I didn't." He smiled at Clare and said kindly, "You were too fast for me."

Clare appreciated the praise but didn't take it seriously. "And?" she prompted.

"Truth be told, I guessed there was a bit of cheating going on. I talked to Vanessa and Ken after. They did some of the science questions and they slipped that one in to help me."

"So you chose not to answer it," Clare surmised. "That was very fair-minded of you, like deliberately missing a penalty that shouldn't have been awarded in the first place. Under the circumstances, we wouldn't have been half so chivalrous."

The lecturer shook his head. "It was more foolish than chivalrous. We'd have won. Still, it's the taking part that counts."

Together, with the same broad smile, Brett and Clare said, "Is it?"

Tim laughed. "No, you're right. I don't believe it either. It's the winning that really counts."

When Brett's mobile phone rang, he growled to Clare, "This had better not be Kosler again."

It wasn't. It was Louise and she said simply, "I suggest you stop at a phone box and give me a call."

"OK," Brett replied. "Give us a few minutes."

While Clare waited on double yellow lines, Brett asked Louise, "What's come up?"

"It's Michael Breach's car again. It's on yesterday's list of cars near the airport – about eight o'clock coming off Parkway at the airport turn."

"Interesting. Thanks, Louise. I think you know where we'll be for a while."

Michael Breach was at home with his wife and baby son. Michael looked as rugged as ever but just as sober. In the large living room, Brett said to him, "We have to ask you where you were yesterday evening, about eight o'clock."

"Eight o'clock? I was..." He glanced at his wife. "I was out with mates, wasn't I, love?"

She nodded. "I would've been as well, if we could've got a baby-sitter."

"Whereabouts did you go?"

"We went to the local," Michael answered. "And, in case you're wondering, I only had a couple."

"This local pub really is local, is it? On this side of town?"

"That's right."

"In that case, Mr Breach, we'd like you to come down to the station with us," Brett said.

Startled, Michael cried, "What? You're arresting me?"

Brett smiled and shook his head. "No, nothing so

dramatic. I'm asking for your help. I'd like you to come and identify some ATC equipment that we've got at headquarters. It's very important to our investigation. We need to know if it belongs to Sheffield City Airport and if it was around when you were there. That sort of thing."

Michael sighed and then shrugged. "All right, I suppose. I'm not exactly busy so … OK." He went for a coat and then kissed his wife goodbye.

Out in the car, before she pulled away, Clare announced, "You know we're being very considerate to you, don't you? Much kinder than we need to be."

"What do you mean?" asked Michael.

"There's nothing to identify," Brett admitted as Clare cruised aimlessly down the road. "We just thought you might want to tell us what's going on without your wife around."

"What do you mean?"

"I mean, if you won't tell us where you were last night right now, we'll have to raise the issue of your relationship with Danielle in front of her."

"My relationship with Danielle?" He appeared to be about to deny it.

"She told us you'd had an affair."

Michael's resistance began to show cracks. His head dropped and he said no more but he mumbled something incoherent to himself.

"First, is it true?"

Michael nodded miserably.

"Let's come back to last night again. Where were

you?" Clare queried.

"I told you." It was a weak response.

In an uncompromising tone, Brett replied, "We've been very sympathetic with you, so we expect your full co-operation. If you were in the local pub, why was your car up near the airport?"

"Ah." Michael realized that he'd been caught out. He swallowed and then muttered, "Did you see me?"

"No," Brett responded. "A camera saw you."

"Damn surveillance. You can't get away from it." Taking a deep breath, he said, "It was Danielle's idea. She called me. She wanted to see me – straight after the eight-fifteen touched down and she'd finished work. I don't know why. Anyway, I didn't see her. Something was going on when I got there."

Interrupting, Brett said pointedly, "Again."

"Yes, again," Michael replied. "Then you two showed up. That proved it – there was definitely something going on – so I got out of there."

"Why did you agree to see her?"

"Well, she did pretty much what you just did. She said she'd tell my wife."

Clare shook her head. "The trouble people get into by being unfaithful." She stopped the car by Millhouses park. On the other side of the hedge a young mother and her toddler were feeding the ducks with crusts. The boy got so excited that he squealed with delight and tottered towards the birds, frightening most of them away. "Why do you think she wanted to see you?"

"No idea. You'd better ask her. But if there was a problem up at the airport, something might cross your minds."

It had already, but Brett asked anyway. "Like what?"

"Well, doesn't it feel strange to you that she was getting me up there exactly when something was going off? It's like she was setting me up by dragging me there at the precise time."

The possibility that Danielle had successfully put Breach in the frame had already occurred to both Brett and Clare. "OK, Michael," Brett said. "That's it for the moment. We can take you home now."

"No," Michael replied quickly. "I'll walk from here. If I get back too soon, it'll look suspicious." He scrambled out and, with relief, closed the door behind him. Then he went slowly into the park.

Before they drove off, Brett said, "Now that Strawberry's targeted Sheffield again, Danielle's got herself on the suspect list, especially because she's implicated Breach." Brett stopped watching Michael and turned to his partner.

"That could be coincidence," Clare replied as she looked in the rear-view mirror.

"Could be. Could be something else. She could be Strawberry, despite her gender."

Clare still didn't believe it but she recognized that they had to consider Danielle as a suspect. "Yeah," she said with a grin. "It'd be the first known case of a gooseberry turning into a Strawberry."

It was getting late and Danielle had already left the airport. Yet Strawberry had given Brett and Clare a deadline. Unless they paid him off at the weekend, he would hit Heathrow in six days. They could not afford the luxury of leaving the case until morning. They got Louise to look up the airport manager's home address. Heading south for Chesterfield, Clare observed, "I reckon we're well and truly back in British mode. It didn't take us long to crush twenty-five hours of work into each day." Then she added, "I don't suppose you're going to bother with the formalities like informing Derbyshire Police about this little incursion into their territory, are you?"

"It's not really worth it, is it?" Brett replied. "It'll only take a few minutes. Besides, we're under radio silence. I can't call them."

"Good excuse."

Danielle was surprised to see the two detectives at the front door of her plush property. "Oh, hello," she muttered. Standing to one side, she said, "Er... I suppose you'd better come in. What's it all about?"

"That's what we wanted to ask you," Brett replied. "What's it all about?"

Genuinely, she seemed perplexed. "What do you mean?"

"You phoned Michael Breach and asked to see him last night, just when you lost navigation."

"Yes. Well. I didn't know when I called that we'd be under siege. How could I?"

Brett and Clare were both thinking the same thing. If she was Strawberry she could be very precise about predicting the next strike. Neither of them responded to her comment. Instead, they sat on the seats that she offered. Brett asked, "Did you see him?"

"No," she answered. "I don't even know if he came. Airport business took over, rather."

"*Why* did you want to see him?"

She stalled for time by repeating Clare's question. "Why did I want to see him? Well, I suppose I wanted to have it out with him. I wanted to see for myself if he was behind this GPS mischief."

Clare was wondering how many detectives there were on this case. Vanessa and Ken were investigating Stefan. Stefan was investigating them. Now, Danielle was investigating Michael Breach. Clare said, "And how were you going to find out if he's our villain?"

"I don't know. I thought I'd look him in the eye and ask if he was trying to ruin my airport. I think I could tell."

"You threatened to speak to his wife."

"That's my right," Danielle snapped at Clare. "You don't know how much he hurt me. I have a right to hurt him back."

"Would you try to hurt him by making it look like he's behind these attacks?"

Danielle opened her mouth and closed it again before answering. "Even if I wanted to, I couldn't."

"Why not?"

"It's obvious. I didn't know when – or if – our navigation was going to be sabotaged."

Brett put in, "Where were you the weekend before last – and Monday the first?"

Taken aback, Danielle cried, "This is crazy! Are you saying I'd sabotage my own airport?"

"We're just establishing where all the players were at certain times," Brett replied.

Still indignant, Danielle answered, "For a change, I had a bit of time off."

"To do what?"

"Work around the house."

"Did you go to the London area?"

Danielle denied it emphatically.

Trying a different angle, Clare asked, "Before you broke up, did Michael tell you all about himself?"

Danielle seemed relieved that the police officers had changed the focus. "Like what?"

"Like, do you know what sort of school he went to?"

"He didn't have to tell me. If I wanted to know, I'd look it up on his cv. I got it when he applied for the job."

"Did you ask how he got on with his school teachers?" It was the sort of information that Danielle would have to know if she was Strawberry and she'd written the e-mail messages in Breach's style to incriminate her ex-boyfriend.

Danielle thought about it for a moment. "I don't think so. It's hardly relevant in a job application."

"But it's the sort of thing two people having an affair might have talked about."

Danielle frowned. "Is it? I think we had better things to do."

Clare asked, "Did you plan to say anything else to him last night?"

"Such as?"

"I don't believe all this stuff about you staring into his eyes and asking about GPS sabotage," Clare replied. "I think you were going to give him an ultimatum. Think again about who you want to live with or your wife gets to hear about it."

Slickly, Danielle avoided a real response. "You've got it into your heads that I'm a vindictive woman, haven't you?"

Clare did not respond. She kept her eyes firmly on Danielle.

"Either way – whatever I was going to say to him

– I'm not going to jeopardize my own airport," she retorted.

It was another night to be spent apart – like all the others. At her club, Clare worked the day out of her system in the swimming pool, gym and then the jacuzzi. Between games of squash, Brett fended off questions about the GPS jamming case from Phil Chapman, his friend and opponent. Brett won the match more easily than usual. It was because he took his frustrations out on that poor innocent little ball, slamming it into the wall mercilessly.

Relaxing in the frothing water, one of Clare's karate mates reminded her, "One time, a few weeks back, you brought a rather gorgeous bloke in with you."

"Brett."

"Yeah. Are you going to bring him in again?"

Clare smiled. "Why?"

"First, tell me, are you still with him?"

"Well, we came to an agreement," Clare replied, trying to keep the regret from her voice. "We decided we were colleagues and nothing more."

"Really?"

Clare nodded. "Yes, that's what we agreed."

"Then you won't mind bringing him in and introducing me to him, will you?"

Clare wondered how she'd feel about Brett going out with someone else. It would be hard but she would not turn vengeful like Danielle. She'd learn to accept it. But somehow she couldn't imagine it happening. He'd be attractive to any woman. He wouldn't be short of offers. But he was also the faithful sort. He'd probably be faithful to her despite the arrangement they'd made on Tobago.

After the game and over a beer, Phil said, "You ought to bring Clare here."

"Why's that?" asked Brett, knowing that his friend still saw himself as a matchmaker.

"For a game of squash. Why else?" Phil replied with a smirk.

"I wouldn't dare," Brett said, side-stepping Phil's implication. "She'd probably beat us both, then how would we feel? It wouldn't do much for our manhood, would it?"

"You're only joking. I can't see her – or anyone else – beating you."

"You haven't seen her in action. I wouldn't be so sure."

Phil leaned forward and squeezed his mate's arm. "When are you going to bow to the inevitable, Brett? You fancy her. In fact, I think you love her."

Brett took a drink to avoid answering. Yes, keeping up a purely professional relationship with Clare was a form of slow torture. And it could only be a matter of time before Clare went out with someone else. Someone like Tim Darke perhaps. After all, she was very attractive and she wouldn't be short of offers. When it happened, Brett would find it intensely painful. He didn't know if he could ever learn to accept it. So, perhaps Phil was right. Certainly, Brett was discovering that it was easy to make an arrangement with Clare on a tropical beach but that afterwards it was much harder to keep, like a New Year resolution.

Early on Wednesday morning, DS Kosler sent out pairs of officers to interview the owners of cars that had appeared on video near the airport when both attempts at sabotage had taken place. He made an exception only for Michael Breach. At one of the networked computers, Stan was protesting to Dennis that Louise was dealing with incoming messages before he had a chance to intervene. She was taking overall control. When Kosler repeated his colleague's complaint for Brett's benefit, Brett did not offer sympathy. "It's not Louise's fault that Stan's always a step behind her."

On cue, Louise announced the arrival of an e-mail from Forensics. "Coming out on the printer now," she said.

Before he went to retrieve the message, Brett nodded at Dennis and commented, "Your man's just not efficient enough to compete with my team."

The memo was an initial report on the forensic examination of the jammer and a list of its component parts. To Clare and Dennis, Brett said, "The outside of the jammer's clean – apart from a bit of soil. No fingerprints."

"Pity," Kosler murmured.

"Perhaps," Brett replied. "But it's significant in itself."

"Is it?" Kosler retorted blankly.

"Absolutely. It means whoever used it was wearing gloves or cleaned the dabs off afterwards. Why would he do that? It's almost as if he thought we might get hold of it and he didn't want to give us a set of prints."

At once, Clare supported her partner. "It strikes me Strawberry's the confident sort. He's not expecting us dumb cops to catch him so he wouldn't bother to keep his jammer free of prints – not unless he wanted us to find it."

"What are you two trying to say?" Kosler uttered. "Are you still going on about someone planting the jammer on Cork?"

"Not necessarily, but it's one possibility," Brett answered. "It certainly explains the lack of prints." Scanning the rest of the report, he added, "It's home-made and its design more-or-less matches the one on that Polish website. Interesting."

This time, Dennis agreed.

"But let's not go dashing off to arrest Rzepinski," Brett said quickly to the Thames Valley man. "We need more on him than this."

"Anything else?" Dennis asked.

"Yes," Brett replied. "The inside. Still no prints or hairs – even though it's home-made. But they found a few things."

"What?"

"The circuit board's held in place by small screws. There's a small scratch on the inner casing, starting from one of the screw heads. That means someone slipped with the screwdriver when they were tightening it."

"How does that help?" Kosler said.

"Somewhere," Brett answered, "there's a small screwdriver with a microscopic trace of paint from the casing. Beige topcoat and white primer. It'd be nice to find it."

"Mmm. Not easy. You can't hope to confiscate every screwdriver of every suspect. Anything else?"

"Debris analysis. They think the inside was vacuum cleaned so they didn't recover much. But they handpicked two tiny fibre fragments stuck to sharp parts. Looks like green polyester, source unknown. They went over the inside with sticky tape and got a few microscopic paint flakes and metal particles. The paint flakes are rounded and grey in colour and the metal – steel according to the scanning electron microscope – is very smooth, both suggesting lots of wear. Source unknown."

"Source unknown," Dennis repeated gloomily.

Clare slapped her partner on the back. "Bet you're feeling better now. You've got worn jeans and a few minuscule particles."

"Yeah. It's not much but it's something to work on."

"At least my raid on Cork's place paid off," Dennis said. "No matter who Strawberry is, now we've got his jammer, his strike on Heathrow's not on the cards."

Clare did not share Kosler's optimism. She replied, "I wouldn't be so sure. If Strawberry's Brendan Cork, yes, it's probably all over because we've unexpectedly taken his toy away."

Kosler interrupted. "And I've tripled his surveillance."

"But," Clare continued, "if Strawberry's someone else, he's framed Cork. That means he's reckoned on sacrificing a jammer. He'll have another – or he'll be making it at this very moment. I'll guarantee it. He's not someone who leaves things to chance. One jammer to frame Cork and another to carry on his crusade. He'll use his back-up at Heathrow."

Wearing the usual Electrics Unlimited T-shirt, Dylan McPhee was sitting at a clean desk in the back room of the shop. Using precision forceps and white nylon gloves, he was sorting delicate chips into plastic boxes.

Brett nodded towards the small pile of components and said, "That's going to extremes to avoid touching them."

"Not at all," Dylan replied. "I'll tell you, one spot of grease from fingers can stop these kiddies working. You see, they take a tiny current. A touch of finger grease on the contacts is enough resistance to stop the current altogether." He put the tweezers down and stripped off the gloves. "What do you want?"

Brett held out the list of parts from the confiscated jammer. "Take a look at those, if you will, and tell me if you've sold them."

Clare added, "Especially if you've sold two of each item to someone."

While he scanned the catalogue, Dylan stroked his chin. "These are pretty much standard issue."

"Even the beige box?"

"Common as muck in this business. They're used for housing all sorts of electrical units."

"Are you saying you could supply all these parts?"

McPhee glanced down the list again. "Not quite all. I'll check it against the computer if you like but I reckon I've got a lot of it in stock right now."

"And do you know who might have bought these items?"

"Do me a favour. I can't keep records and I don't have an impossibly good memory."

"How about the man with the Stetson hat?" Brett prompted.

Dylan nodded. "Possibly. I really don't know. But after you left last time, I remembered he'd bought a starter for an old lawnmower. At least I think that was him."

Trying to help McPhee's dubious powers of recall, Clare asked, "What about Mr Nash? Do you think he bought anything on this list?"

"Erm… Let me think. I had to order some things for him. What were they? Yes. I do believe one or two might be here but I couldn't swear to it. Come to think of it, there might be more than one or two but, before you ask, my computer records won't help. I can look up what I've ordered but there's too much to keep a record of who wanted it. After it's been collected, we lose the customer's name."

Aware that Strawberry could be putting a jammer together right now, Clare asked, "Has anyone been in for parts like these yesterday or first thing this morning?"

Dylan shook his head. "Maybe a few of them but that'll just be coincidence. They're common components. No one's been in for all this lot. I wish they had. It'd come to a tidy sum."

Brett thought they'd pushed McPhee as far as they could. Instead he said, "By the way, what do you do with the big aerial you've got out the back?"

"It's obvious, isn't it? Sheffield's in such a hole, reception's bad to dreadful so it's there in case someone wants us to demonstrate a radio picking up Russian radio broadcasts."

"I see." Then Brett asked, "Do you keep in touch with teachers at your old school?"

"What?" Dylan was taken aback by the question.

"Well? Do you?"

"No. They never really had any interest in me. Why should I take an interest in them? Besides, it was a long time ago. Half of them will be dead by now, I should think."

"Why were you expelled from the grammar school?"

"What is this? Some sort of inquisition?"

Brett repeated the question.

Dylan sighed before answering, "This can't have anything to do with your investigation. Let's just say I was a bit too lively for them. I didn't just want to jump through their hoops. I wanted to make things, use a bit of imagination. And I took a few things to help me."

"You sound like you might bear a grudge."

"Maybe once," said Dylan. "But it was ages ago. You can't let these things eat you away. Besides, I guess I *was* a bit of a handful."

"Were you here in the shop a week last Saturday and Monday the first?"

"Where else would I be?" Dylan responded, losing the last dregs of his patience.

"Will your staff confirm that?"

McPhee snapped with absolute certainty, "Of course they will."

Of course they would. Either Dylan McPhee was innocent and he had been serving in his hectic shop, or he was guilty and he had told his workers to swear he had not gone anywhere. No doubt, they would agree to cover up his absence if they valued their jobs.

On the way out, apparently by accident, Brett brushed against one of McPhee's helpers. That way, he transferred a few fibres from the green T-shirt on to his own jacket. In the car, he dabbed at the point of contact with a piece of sticky tape that he had brought for the purpose. The analysis of the fibres could prove very interesting.

Stefan Rzepinski put on a brilliant little-boy-lost act – or maybe he really was. He had travelled alone to another country and was wrestling not just with the pressure of a university course but also with a foreign language. He looked like a fish out of water.

Speaking almost in a whisper, he told Brett and Clare what he had learned by eavesdropping on his fellow students. "They are talking much about localizers and GPS."

Clare nodded. "We know they were making up questions on localizer beams and we're not surprised they chat about GPS. It's not every day people get caught up in a police investigation. They're bound to natter about it when they do. As far as we're concerned, Vanessa and Ken aren't under suspicion." She hesitated and then said, "Besides, I thought you were leaving the detective work to the detectives."

"Me?" Stefan smiled coyly. "I am already buying the transmitter. I am having to use it."

Clare could not help but return his boyish grin. She had not received a complaint about his misconduct so she decided not to pursue it but she warned him to be careful. Then she asked, "Where were you on Monday night?"

"Here," he answered. "In the university."

"All the time?"

"Yes."

"You were working very late," Clare observed.

Stefan nodded. "I am in England to work."

"Do you belong to any organizations in Poland?"

"Pardon?"

"Are you a member of any clubs back home?"

He paused, "Only The Physics Society."

"Nothing like a cult?"

"No."

Standing in the electronics laboratory, Brett fingered the small roll of tape in his pocket as Clare continued with the interview. He also counted five small screwdrivers left out on the bench. As Kosler had pointed out, it was ludicrous to seize every one he saw. And what about all those that he couldn't see? There were probably many more out of sight in the cupboards and cabinets.

"Do you keep in touch with friends in Poland?" Clare enquired.

"By e-mail and Internet, yes. There is a good

website for the Polish citizens in foreign counties. It keeps me in touch with news and people."

"Why did you log on to a Polish cult's website?"

"I am doing that because the others do it."

Clare pictured herself going round in a circle for ever. She wasn't getting anywhere so she decided to drop it. Suddenly, though, she wondered if Strawberry's antics were simply an extreme case of attention-seeking. She could imagine that a displaced young man like Stefan might seek attention. "You must feel isolated in England," she said to him.

"Everyone is being very kind to me. I am enjoying it here. But," he admitted, "I do miss home and friends very much."

"You said you wanted to become a forensic scientist," Brett put in. "Do you want to follow that career here or back in Poland?"

"If I am able, I am wanting to make my fortune in England before I return."

Both Brett and Clare were thinking that a million pounds was quite a fortune.

Clare asked him, "Did you have anything to do with GLONASS: the satellite navigation system developed in Poland?"

"I think it is made mainly in Russia. I am working for three months in an institute where they help its making. In my undergraduate course, it is my…"

"Work experience?" Clare suggested.

"Yes. But I work on a different project."

While Clare continued to distract the research

student by talking to him, Brett dragged the sticky side of the tape along the work surface by his computer keyboard. The area was virtually spotless but Brett was hoping that he might be lucky enough to snare a few tiny fibres from a green sweatshirt that he had once seen Stefan wearing.

After talking to Stefan, Brett and Clare went into Dr Darke's office. This time the young lecturer did not get to his feet or shake their hands. Instead he chuckled and said, "This is getting to be a habit. I hope you haven't come to gloat over your victory." He waved them towards the two seats.

"No," Clare retorted in good humour. "We wouldn't want to remind you that you academics were beaten by mere police officers."

Brett tried to ignore their rapport. He found it strangely unsettling. He also tried to ignore the way that Tim looked at his partner. Before he sat down, he handed the list of electronic parts to Tim. "It's just a quick visit. What do you make of those?"

Tim thought about it for a while. "You could make quite a bit out of this little lot but, because it's you, I imagine you reckon it's made a GPS jammer."

Brett nodded. "How much of this would be in your department?"

"The laboratory manager could cross-check it against departmental orders. Do you want me to get him to do that?"

"Yes, please."

"OK. Hang on a moment." He left the office with

the list. He returned after a minute and said, "He'll give us a shout when he's done."

"While we wait, what's your best guess?"

"I imagine we don't have them all – but most." He hesitated before saying, "This means you're thinking someone here might have built it."

Brett replied with a question. "Who'd come closest to using all those components in their research work?"

"I suppose it'd be Stefan," Tim said. "But I don't think you should read anything into that. Most of those items have multiple uses. They don't only go into a GPS jammer. They're like building bricks. You could make something perfectly ordinary out of them. Believe me, Stefan's work's innocent enough. Besides, he's also used a huge number of components that aren't on your list."

"What's Stefan like?" Clare asked. "He seems very meek and mild. And homesick."

Dr Darke smiled. "Don't be fooled by his struggle with the language. You have to be tough to get through a PhD in a foreign country. He's determined and very clever. That's why I took him on. I admire him. As for being homesick, I'd say he was very devoted to his friends and family back home. He'd do anything for them, but he wants his PhD, job experience and some money first."

"How's his *written* English?" Clare was aware that there seemed to be a great gulf between Strawberry's finely crafted e-mails and Stefan's faltering grammar.

"It's better than his spoken language because he

has time to think and look words up but it's hardly perfect."

None of Strawberry's letters had hinted at extreme beliefs but Clare asked, "Does he indulge in any strange behaviour, like he was in some weird organization or cult?"

"Not that I've noticed. He hasn't got a funny free-mason handshake or anything."

Clare grinned. "Glad to hear it," she said.

After a few more minutes, the laboratory manager put his head around the door and announced that eighty per cent of the components on the list had passed through his hands in the last year. A large number of them had been ordered by Stefan Rzepinski.

Back at headquarters, Brett went to Strawberry's *Other* column. Under *Suppliers*, he added *Department of Electronics, Technology Faculty, the university*.

Kosler's officers had not come up with any worthwhile new leads by interviewing the drivers who had been in the region of the airport on both Friday afternoon and Monday evening. Looking at Brett as if he were responsible for a waste of time, Dennis asked, "Do you really think Strawberry's likely to risk using his own car near the airport? He'll know all about video surveillance."

Standing behind Louise, Brett replied, "That's a good point. To be sure, he might leave his own car at home."

"So, if he went near the airport, how could he get there? You're the local advisor."

Ignoring the aggressive tone, Brett thought about it for a moment. "Lots of ways. The bus service isn't exactly reliable but a bus is still a possibility. Maybe he biked, walked, used a taxi. Or even a hired car."

Clare interjected, "Would he carry the jammer on a bike? It's not impossible, I guess."

"No, not impossible but a bit unlikely, especially if it's in a briefcase."

Before they could bring Louise into the conversation, she said, "All right. I'll get on to taxi and car-hire companies."

"Thanks," Brett said. "With hire cars, check if the same person hired one around Saturday 30th August to Monday 1st September for that London trip."

Stan was sitting at another computer, staring at Dennis Kosler, still waiting for orders.

"You know," Brett said thoughtfully, "I feel like a pinball. I'm bouncing between Brendan Cork, Michael Breach, Stefan, Danielle, Tim Darke, Forensics, and Dylan McPhee. I'm getting more points at each bounce – from a suspect or an expert – but I don't seem to be winning the game."

"There'll be a jackpot post somewhere but we haven't crashed into it yet," Clare replied.

Brett said, "We need to take the game by surprise with an unconventional move. If only we could think of one."

Now that DI Lawless and Sergeant Tilley had got so close to him, Strawberry felt a welcome surge of adrenalin throughout his body. It was like being back at school and finding that there *was* a suitable challenge after all. Unexpectedly it had come in the shape of a brawny policeman. Strawberry had no doubt that he was still in control, still on top of the situation, but he was having to be more careful. The game had moved to a higher level. Excellent.

It would not be long before he became a very rich man, courtesy of a bit of science and a lot of imagination. Lawless had made it necessary for him to be even more imaginative than he had anticipated, but he had figured out a new plan. He would have the ransom money, someone else would take the rap and, most satisfying of all, GPS would be utterly discredited. He could imagine the powers-that-be panicking already. They had jumped into bed with the Global Positioning System before they realized that it was not all it was cracked up to be. They were discovering its vulnerability to sabotage only now – when it was too late to change their minds. Fools.

He closed his eyes contentedly and thought his way through the end play again. He needed to be absolutely sure that his scheme for collecting the money was infallible. "Sweet move," he murmured to himself. He believed that he could rely on Kosler to muscle in on the action and behave exactly as he would predict. OK, Strawberry had a lot of work to do on the Internet and a little more manipulation of e-mail, but that was all. The rest would be easy.

22

On Thursday morning, four days before the lethal attack that Strawberry had promised, Brett slid open one of the drawers of a steel filing cabinet. He was about to grab the document that he wanted when his eye was caught by a small accumulation of dirt in the corner of the drawer. He examined the slider mechanism. It had worn a slight groove in the grey paint of the steel drawer through frequent opening and closing. It was likely that the debris consisted of small particles of paint and metal eroded by friction. "Louise," he called. "Get me a little strip of sticky tape, will you?"

He dabbed at the dust and a lot of the particles stuck to it. But they were far too small to explore by eye. Instead he dashed to Forensics with his precious piece of sticky tape, smudged with dirt.

Handing it over to Greta, he said, "Can you compare these particles with the paint and metal you found in the jammer?"

Greta peered at the specimen and asked, "Where did they come from?"

"My filing cabinet."

"Oh?" She slipped the contaminated tape carefully into an evidence bag.

"It's the junk at the bottom of one drawer, under the slider of the one above."

Greta nodded. "You think Strawberry might have stored the jammer in a metal cabinet while he was putting it together and a bit of erosion dust fell into the casing."

"If I'm right it doesn't narrow things down much but it's another piece of the jigsaw."

"I'll let you know this afternoon."

"Anything for me now?"

"You might say I've got more on wear and tear, but jeans this time. I finished the background research and we definitely have a new forensic method. Send me suspects' jeans, or photos of them, and I'll tell you if they belong to the person coming out of the wood – with a high degree of confidence."

"Great. Have you already had a go at the ones Kosler's team sent in?"

"Yes, but no match yet." Greta continued, "We're getting somewhere with the comparison of fibres as well. The Electrics Unlimited T-shirt didn't quite match the green fibres in the jammer. And the sample you got from the university was pretty poor, I'm afraid. We only found one piece of green polyester fibre. That's not enough for a valid comparison."

Brett expected her to say more. "But?" he prompted.

"Bear in mind it's not statistically significant, Brett, but it did match. That's off the record. The source of both sets of fibres could be the same. *Could be*," she stressed. "Without more fibres and more analysis I can't be definite."

"Thanks," Brett replied. "I'll bear it in mind. Could be." It meant Stefan Rzepinski could be Strawberry. If so, perhaps he'd had help to write the electronic letters. An idea began to form in Brett's mind.

Louise's results from car hire and taxi firms were disappointing. "I've had no joy from car hire places," she reported, "unless Strawberry's, you know, got a false driving licence so I'm looking for the wrong names."

"Taxis?"

"I've got a few who delivered people to the airport or thereabouts at the right times but their record-keeping is ... how shall I put it?"

"Atrocious?"

"Yes," Louise replied. "Very few names, and none of them are the ones we want to hear."

Dennis said, "Just in case, I'll put a couple of men on to questioning the ones you have got."

"You could send someone round to Stefan

Rzepinski's place to get fibres from all his clothing, especially a green sweatshirt," Brett put in. "We could go but he might feel more pressure if someone else – someone he doesn't know – breathes down his neck this time."

"There's a problem, though," Clare said. "Even if Greta confirms a match, it's circumstantial."

"Yes," Brett agreed. "It'd prove Rzepinski was near the jammer when it was made. That wouldn't convict him. It doesn't even prove he made it, never mind used it. But, given the choice, I'd prefer to know who was around when it was made than not know anything. It'd tell us we're closing in on the target. I can sort out a photographer to go with them. Then, we can get shots of all his pairs of jeans at the same time. That might just help, but… Anyway, I won't pre-judge the results. Let's see what the photos tell us." Brett turned to Dennis and asked, "You contacted Gatwick about Brendan Cork, didn't you?"

"Ages ago."

"Time to talk to them again," Brett announced. "I wonder if Cork warned anyone in the airport business about over-reliance on GPS – or whether he had anything to do with it at all – before he was made redundant as a flight engineer." Brett switched the phone so the conversation would be relayed by a loudspeaker to the whole incident room.

"Stan," Kosler shouted. "Get me that Gatwick technical number, will you?"

On the other end of a noisy line, the supervisor at Gatwick Airport groaned. "Brendan Cork." Then he sighed as if he was being asked to relive a painful episode. "Cork had opinions on everything, you understand. You name it, he was rude about it – over and over again. Customs procedures, his colleagues, aircraft maintenance, GPS, everything."

"GPS?" Kosler queried.

"Global Positioning System."

"I know what it is, see?" Dennis retorted. "I was asking what he said about it."

"Sorry, I'm sure," the supervisor replied, making it plain that he did not like the superintendent's manner.

Listening in, Brett was thinking the same. He wished that he was asking the questions but it was Kosler's home territory.

The Gatwick engineer continued, "I'd summarize Cork's attitude like this. If the old system ain't broke, why fix it? He saw dangers in relying on weak signals from satellites that are here today and possibly knocked out by a bit of space debris tomorrow. He saw them as a showy, expensive, high-profile replacement for solid ground-based beacons. To a degree, he was right. What's wrong with upgrading old technology, as opposed to always inventing a fancy new one? Not sexy enough, I suppose. But if a beacon on the ground goes off-line, someone can take a stroll and fix it. You can't take a stroll to a satellite."

"So, Cork definitely didn't approve of GPS."

"He objected to all sorts of things. Often his gripes seemed to be a way of showing off his knowledge and superiority. Let's put it this way. We weren't devastated to see the back of him. Constant harping isn't the way to make friends and influence people."

"OK. Thanks." Kosler put the phone down and declared, "That's another nail in Cork's coffin. He's our man. I'm convinced."

Brett nodded. He wasn't really agreeing but he was beginning to see how Cork might fit into the picture. "But," he said to Dennis, "how are you going to prove it?"

"Bits of fibre and metal aren't going to do the job," Kosler replied, decrying Brett's forensic approach. "We need something heavy duty. I know what it'll come down to. We'll get him with a trap when he collects the fake money, see? There's nothing wrong with old-fashioned police work."

"Like old-fashioned ground-based beacons," Brett said.

"Exactly."

"But you tried a traditional trap and it didn't work," Brett pointed out. "We need a hi-tech tactic for a hi-tech crook."

"Rubbish," Kosler replied. "We'll learn from last time. We'll use a better bug, be more careful."

"I'll tell you what we learned from last time. He's too clever," Brett insisted. "He'll detect any bug. He'll sniff it out somehow."

"So," Kosler said, "what do we do, according to you?"

"We haven't got long to find him so we keep going. We're beginning to latch on to good leads. But if we do get into a ransom situation, we go fishing with real money and we don't use electronics."

"What have you got in mind, Brett?" asked Clare, trying to take the sting out of the exchange.

"I'm not a hundred per cent sure yet. But a lot of scientists know all about their own field and not a great deal outside it. I need to make a call to Derek Jacob at the university because I'm wondering about a chemical tag."

"Strawberry'll see it," Kosler snorted. "It'll be more obvious than a tiny hidden bug."

"Not the one I'm thinking of," Brett said. "An invisible one. We might be able to put an indelible fluorescent marker on the handle of whatever bag or case he tells us to use. It'll be invisible in ordinary light. When he picks the bag up, some of the stuff'll transfer to his hand. Later, it'll show up under ultraviolet light."

Clare nodded. "Like those security pens for writing your name and postcode invisibly on property just before it gets nicked."

Brett nodded. "That's the one."

"Sounds dodgy to me," Dennis replied. "And I'd like to see you convince your chief to use real money, especially when you're thinking of letting Strawberry walk off with it and you just hope you catch up with him afterwards — with shiny stuff on his fingers. Macfarlane'll throw a fit."

"He might, yes, but Strawberry'll examine the money at the drop-site. He's bound to. And if he thinks it's dud, he'll be off with his jammer. Using fakes is too much of a gamble."

"Your way, there's a big risk we'll lose a million."

"Better that than lives."

"The money's not important to you, is it?" Kosler said. "It's just a hook to catch Strawberry."

"Exactly," Brett replied. "Now we've got our priorities sorted out, I'd better talk to John because he'll need some warning. It'll take time to put together a million."

Clare said, "Easy. He'll just take it out of your wages this month, Brett."

"**A** million!" Big John cried. "And where do you expect me to raise that kind of cash? Do I take it out of my salary?"

Brett smiled. "I don't know, but I do know it's too dangerous to mess with Strawberry again. He'll smell any fakes or bugs. We don't want him to suss it out and go down south in a mood."

John Macfarlane sighed. "You're right – and Strawberry's right – about one thing. Unless you lot pull your fingers out and get him today or tomorrow, we'll have to give him the money at the weekend. We can't let him loose on Heathrow. It'd be a total disaster."

"We could still lay out counterfeit cash," Kosler said. "I've got my boys back at home working on convincing fakes and an undetectable bug."

"Successfully?"

"Not yet," Dennis admitted.

"Are they going to deliver before the weekend?"

The Thames Valley man could only shrug.

John looked at Clare.

She said, "I reckon Strawberry's much too good to miss a trick. I've got a feeling he'll be able to detect even an undetectable bug and spot dummy notes. I wouldn't put it past him to be monitoring bank activity electronically. He might know if we've taken the money out."

John nodded slowly and came to his decision. "OK. Here it is. One: you carry on nailing him before he demands the cash. Two: I'll work on the contingency plan – just in case. We'll lure him with real money. I'll need to stump it up and sort out insurance. It'll take time and a lot of serious persuasion."

"And we let him walk away with it," Brett added. "No electronic bug."

Kosler shook his head vigorously. "We can't let him take that much. We've got to collar him on the spot and, in case he gets through the net, use a bug in the money."

"Too chancy," Brett argued. "We let him think he's beaten us. He'll relax more if he thinks he's got away with it. That's when we step in and arrest him."

"How?" Big John enquired.

"I phoned my old chemistry tutor up the road at the university. He agrees we can tag a bag and the money with an indelible fluorescent chemical marker. After the pick-up, we go to our suspects with a UV light and catch them red-handed. Actually, it's more likely to be blue-handed."

"Let me think about that one, Brett," John replied. "I see the risk with a bug but I'm not sure our insurers'll jump up and down with joy at the idea of letting him disappear into the sunset with all that cash."

"The tag'll show up better in the dark," Brett said with a grin.

Greta confirmed it by telephone. "The particles in your own filing cabinet were general muck with a few steel shards, but mainly smooth paint flakes. And, yes, they're almost identical to the fragments inside the jammer. You've got yourself a theory, Brett. When this jammer was being made it might have been kept in the drawer of a metal filing cabinet – and not a new one at that. It must have seen a bit of wear to start shedding paint like that." In an ironic tone, she said, "All you've got to do is find an old grey filing cabinet and you've got your culprit."

"Thanks again, Greta. That's helpful."

"Best of luck with it."

On the way to Hill Top with a photograph of Stefan Rzepinski, Clare stopped the car and turned to her partner. "Hadn't you better tell me what's on your mind? I can tell something's brewing."

"We ought to find some time for ourselves, Clare," he replied. "At least, that's what *I* think we need to do. It's easy to adjust to the weather but it's not so easy to adjust back to our old working relationship." He looked into her face and said, "I still... Anyway, we need to talk."

Clare nodded. "OK. I know what you mean. If the case lets us, we could get together one evening. You could cook me one of your veggie meals."

"Yeah." Brett smiled. "That sounds good to me."

Clare pulled out of the lay-by and said, "There's something else."

"I want to know if Brendan Cork's going to admit to knowing Stefan."

"Got you," Clare replied at once. "Your imagination's been on the job again. And it makes sense. Cork's got another air-band radio and on Monday he listens to air traffic transmissions. That way, he knows when the plane's coming in to land. He calls Stefan at the university and gets him to switch on the jammer. No need for Stefan to leave the campus to make a strike. You're thinking Strawberry might be a couple of people."

"That's not all," Brett added. "It also explains why the e-mails were so well written. Stefan had a writer to do them for him. On top of that, Stefan's lab is riddled with old grey cabinets."

Clare nodded. "The motives are OK as well. Stefan could be doing it on behalf of some cult with a campaign against the West. Tim Darke said he'd do anything to help out the folks back home. That's how I read him as well. He's lonely and gullible. Cork's proving he was right about GPS."

"It's a convenient relationship."

Inside Brendan's comfortable cottage, Brett held out the photograph of Stefan Rzepinski and asked, "Do you know this man?"

Clare watched Brendan carefully as he looked at the picture and then denied it. He showed no signs of lying. Perhaps he was good at it. Perhaps he didn't know Stefan. Perhaps, if they were partners, they had never met but used only electronic communication.

Brett carried on with the interview. "I don't have a search warrant, I admit, but do you have a metal filing cabinet in the house?"

"I'm afraid you've come up here for nothing," Brendan replied haughtily.

"What does that mean?"

"It means I haven't got one. Full stop. I left all that sort of thing back at Gatwick. No more filing for me. As a writer, I'm allowed to be disorganized and scatty. It's part of the job description."

"Are you sure? Remember, I can apply for a search warrant."

Brendan opened his arms in a gesture of honesty. "You can look now if you want. I haven't got one."

"All right." It was the answer that Brett had been expecting. He believed that Cork had bought only lawnmower parts and maybe other harmless items from Electrics Unlimited. He believed that Cork did not have anything to do with the jammer – not even the one that had been buried in his garden. Someone had surely put it there to incriminate him. If Stefan was his partner, perhaps there was a power struggle between them. Stefan could be trying to shift the blame entirely on to Brendan Cork. Maybe Stefan intended to take the ransom money while Cork took the rap. Tim Darke had said that his research student was very clever.

Next, it was Stefan Rzepinski's turn to deny all knowledge of Brendan Cork. But, as soon as he had said it in his curious English, his gaze shifted back to the photograph. "Yes?" Clare said, wondering if he was going to change his mind.

"Maybe I am seeing him. His hat is..." Stefan smiled. "Crazy, you know. Maybe I know it. I am thinking to see him in a shop somewhere."

"Electrics Unlimited?"

Stefan shrugged. "Perhaps."

The student's slow and stilted speech gave him plenty of time to consider his responses. The fact that he looked uncomfortable with the questions meant nothing. Stefan was uncomfortable with the English language anyway.

He returned the snapshot. With eyes moving from Clare to Brett, he enquired, "Why do people look at my clothes?"

For a moment, Brett wondered what the student was talking about. Then he realized that Stefan was referring to Kosler's officers. Brett explained, "You said you were into forensic science. The first principle of forensic science is that when two things come into contact with each other, there's always a transfer of material between them. We're finding out whose clothes have come into contact with a GPS jammer." He decided to be open about his reasoning to put pressure on Stefan if he was guilty. "Do you want to save us doing the analysis by telling us if you've made or used a GPS jammer?"

"No."

"You mean, you don't want to tell us or you haven't?"

"I am not jamming," Stefan stated bluntly.

Later, Clare said to Brett, "This idea of two people being involved throws up all sorts of possibilities. It's not just Cork and Stefan. Brendan Cork could have been in contact with any one of a number of people – even Vanessa Street and Ken Price, right under our noses."

"Yes," Brett agreed. "They could've pushed the button during the quiz. We wouldn't have known."

"There was a lot of button-pushing going on in the quiz," Clare reminded him. "Especially mine. Anyway, Vanessa and Ken set up the whole thing. You don't think they rigged up more than a buzzer system, do you?"

"You mean, they fixed it so one of the buzzers activated the jammer? I wouldn't have thought so. It'd be a bit random."

"It might be the reason Tim Darke didn't go for

his buzzer on the localizer question. Maybe it was too soon to turn the jammer on."

Brett smiled. "How many people do you think are hiding behind Strawberry? Tim Darke as well? I reckon he's still out of it. He couldn't have taken a message from Cork or anyone else. He was listening to quiz questions."

"Unless he was wired and we didn't see it."

"Now you're just guessing. Let's work it out from the evidence."

Clare looked at her watch. "We could do it over that meal you promised me. Then we could talk about … other things."

"It's a deal."

But it didn't happen. Louise called them back to the incident room. An untraceable e-mail had arrived from Strawberry. Brett and Clare went in to study Strawberry's instructions on exactly how and where they were to hand over the money.

24

While he read Strawberry's instructions, Brett smiled at the man's cunning. He wanted the money buried on Saturday afternoon at an exact location on the peak of Win Hill, west of Sheffield. Cheekily, Strawberry suggested that they could pinpoint the place with a GPS position indicator. He was avoiding a dangerous person-to-person hand-over, obviously intending to collect the ransom secretly at some time between Saturday afternoon and Monday morning. The plan would allow him to examine the money carefully, making sure it was genuine and free of bugs, before walking away with it – or leaving it behind and committing multiple murder instead.

"Where is this Win Hill?" Dennis Kosler queried. "Is it near Hill Top? It sounds like it."

"Not really. It's a few miles further out – into Derbyshire. There's Hallam Moor in between," Brett told him. "Win Hill overlooks Ladybower Reservoir. Very nice. It's also a nifty spot for a drop-site. No roads, just a steep walk up through some woods. It's not the most popular walk in the area either so it's usually deserted. His grid reference is way above the tree line so we can't sneak surveillance cameras among the trees. In fact, it's very exposed and desolate up there. Last time I went up, I nearly got blown off the top. There's no hiding place. Strawberry'll see everything at a glance. This time, he's made sure we won't have cars, people, cameras or any heavy equipment in the vicinity."

"You're enjoying this!" Kosler snapped.

"No," Brett replied. "But I appreciate his thinking. He's a step ahead. Till we spring our fluorescent surprise."

"Mmm. Well, he's made it clear he appreciates you as well," Dennis muttered. Plainly, Strawberry's previous message was still playing on his mind.

To get Kosler off his back for a while, Brett said, "I suggest you take a car and walking boots – you'll need good ones – and hike up Win Hill yourself tomorrow. That way, you'll see what you're up against, and you'll appreciate Strawberry's smart choice as well. Besides," he added, "it's a pity to come all this way up the M1 and not see some of our hills. I know you don't have such things down south."

"Maybe."

They gathered round an OS map and, well into the evening, planned their tactics.

On Friday, Greta's e-mail surprised Brett. Just as he was beginning to feel that he was on top of the game, his favourite forensic scientist bowled an unplayable delivery. *None of the fibres from Rzepinski's clothes provide a clear match with the polyester fragments from inside the electronic jamming device. The wear patterns on Rzepinski's jeans do not match that of the individual code-named Bowden Housteads.*

Clare groaned. She looked towards Brett and said, "Perhaps Kosler's team didn't get samples from all his gear."

"Perhaps." Brett shook his head in disappointment.

"If Stefan's that good, he might have got rid of the clothes he wore when he made the jammer. That'd be clever and cautious – just in case he'd left a clue."

"I know. But I think something's still not quite right about it. There might be another explanation."

"Oh?"

Brett said, "If it was Stefan who buried the jammer, he was trying to manipulate and confuse us. We were meant to find it so it's not helpful. I thought we had three clues he didn't mean us to have: Bowden's jeans, the filing cabinet bits, and the fibres. They're the ones he doesn't know we've got, where *we're* in control. But now I'm worried in case he planted the fibres and debris as well. That'd mean we were meant to find them and they'll mislead us.

Then we'd be back to only one worthwhile piece of evidence. But Bowden might have nothing to do with it. That'd send us back to square one without a clue."

"You *do* think he's smart, don't you?"

"Stefan's admitted he's into forensic science. That'd help him pull the wool over our eyes."

"Yeah," Clare replied. "He plants fibres from someone else's clothes in the jammer. Maybe Cork's. No," she corrected herself. "It would *have* to be Cork's. If he's trying to put the blame on someone else, he wouldn't frame two different people. That would be pointless and daft. He'd just go for the one: Brendan Cork."

"Unless?" Brett prompted.

Clare thought about it and then replied, "Unless he's just playing with us."

Brett nodded. "It's a possibility. The fallout from a grey filing cabinet doesn't tie in with Cork so Strawberry might have a fancy plan involving two people – and one of them's got the grey cabinet."

"You don't know for sure Strawberry did plant the traces in the jammer. They could be straightforward leads."

"True. That's what I'm hoping, but we can't rely on it." Brett paused and said, "Now more than ever, we don't know if Stefan's Strawberry, or one half of Strawberry, or perfectly innocent."

Clare looked at her watch. Ominously, she commented, "We've got thirty hours to find out."

"Yes. I'm beginning to think we'll have to dish out

the money before we get him," Brett replied. "Big John's given us the go-ahead to use a fluorescent marker so I'll get Security on to it."

"I guess this means I'm going to miss the match tomorrow," Clare complained.

"It doesn't matter," Brett said. "Wednesday'll never take two on the trot. They've had their win for this year."

With the Forensic Department on standby, Brett and Clare spent the rest of Friday rushing around and gathering samples of green fibres from suspects. But they didn't find a match with the traces in the jammer. Brendan Cork's clothing, Danielle's office carpet and samples from Michael Breach's house all drew a blank.

Brett and Clare finally slowed down when John Macfarlane announced that he had assembled the money. A million pounds in used fifty- and twenty-pound notes arrived in the incident room with two armed guards and a security technician. One of the guards strained under the weight of the suitcase as he lifted it on to a table.

Taking a deep breath, John flicked open the lid of the suitcase to reveal twenty-five piles of used notes, banded together. There was a reverent hush except for Louise's low whisper, "Wow!" Then there was a moment of silence as if they were in the presence of something more precious than thirty thousand small pieces of soiled paper.

Breaking the spell, Brett said, "OK. Let's get the suitcase and top piles painted with the chemical tag."

The technician stepped forward with a spray gun loaded with a clear liquid.

While he sprayed the invisible dye carefully into every crevice, Louise murmured, "I've never seen that much money before. I never even wondered what it would look like. You know, a whole suitcase. That's a lot of dosh."

"Done," the technician announced, closing the lid and standing back.

"Right," Brett said. "We need a volunteer to test it. Come on, Louise. Haven't you always wanted to hold a million pounds?"

"Me?" She shrunk away as if she'd just been invited to dance by a man she loathed.

"Why not? You can become an instant millionaire for a minute."

"What do you want me to do?"

"Just pick up the case with one hand then fiddle with some of the money with the other. Then we take you into a darkened room and check you're marked on both hands as the thief."

Nervously, Louise stepped forward, took hold of the handle and tried to lift the suitcase. At first, nothing happened. "That's heavy!" she exclaimed. Then, using more strength, she lifted it up for a moment with her right arm.

"OK," Brett told her. "That's enough. You don't have to run off with it."

Relieved, she let it drop back on to the table. "Phew! I couldn't," she replied.

"Open it up and put your left hand on some of the notes."

After she'd done it, she went with Brett and the technician into their first incident room. Without windows, the place became utterly black when Brett switched off the lights.

"I'm turning the ultraviolet lamp on," the technician said.

Suddenly, like something from a weird theatre show, both of Louise's hands came to ghostly life. Her fingers and palms glowed an eerie blue as if they had an alien existence all of their own. She gasped in surprise and held them up, fascinated. In the dark, they seemed to be detached from her. She clenched her fists and the light blue glow almost disappeared. She opened them again and twisted her hands as if she were testing that they really belonged to her. "Amazing."

"Excellent. You're nicked."

Some spots on the technician's clothing glowed like stars as well – where he had been spattered by the spray.

With the electric lights back on, Louise blinked and examined her hands. They looked perfectly normal and clean. She asked the security technician, "Am I marked for life?"

He smiled. "No. But it won't come off. It'll take about two weeks to fade. That's because the skin'll be replaced." He turned to Brett, gave him the hand-held UV lamp and remarked, "That's how long you've got to find your man."

"Let's check again," Brett said, keen to prove to himself that nothing could go wrong. "You go to the Ladies, Louise, and have a good scrub with soap and water. Then I'll scan you again."

But washing did not remove the dye. Louise's hands still shone like detached phantoms.

"All right," Brett said. "I'm convinced. Let's go back."

Once Big John had signed numerous forms to acknowledge that he had received the fortune and would return it after a few days, the visitors left them with the cash. John looked around the room and said, "Into the safe with this till tomorrow."

Kosler asked, "How are we going to get it up the hill? Via helicopter?"

John frowned. "What? So Strawberry can wait till it's dropped the money and then use our one and only chopper as target practice for his jammer? No chance. Besides, it's out there on patrol, chasing the bad guys, monitoring traffic or football fans. No, someone's got to lug the money up the hill. Someone who's seriously fit. It's going to be a long, hard slog."

They all turned and looked at Brett.

It was quiet. Most of the squad had gone home for the evening. Louise remained at her computer and, every now and then, scrutinized her apparently unblemished hands. Brett sat at a desk, coffee cup in hand, and examined the wall charts yet again. Perhaps this time, the answer wasn't written in black and white in front of him but he read through the details once more as if it might be there.

He jumped when Clare tapped him on the shoulder. "It's not helping," she observed. "How about going back to your place for that postponed meal?"

Brett sighed and then nodded. He sighed because he did not have the evidence to identify Strawberry and he nodded because he welcomed an evening off with Clare. "Good idea," he replied. "I'm not getting very far here."

"I just need to do something at home first," Clare said. "There's a radio programme on tonight I don't want to miss. You'll think it's boring: poetry. I'll set my cassette player to record it automatically."

At once, they looked at each other in surprise. Suddenly, they both realized that Clare had stumbled upon something vital.

"You've got a mains timer switch at home," Brett uttered, getting to his feet.

Clare nodded thoughtfully.

Brett said, "Me too. I've got timers so my lights come on if I'm not there."

"So we've both got them. Us and lots of others." She paused before adding, "I think we've been overlooking something, Brett."

Louise turned to Brett and Clare and asked, "Why does a mains timer make any difference?"

"It's Monday night we're worried about," Brett replied. "We've been looking at who was where and what they were doing, whether they were near the airport or in line with the runway. But Strawberry might have set up the jammer on a timer. He could have been anywhere, doing anything."

"But how would he know when the plane was landing?" Louise objected.

"Maybe, before he went wherever he went, he phoned for an expected time of arrival. If he checked that the flight had taken off from Amsterdam on time – six-thirty, British time – he'd assume it'd make the flight without a hitch and set up the jammer on a timer switch for a few minutes before touch-down.

Remember he didn't do any damage on Monday. Maybe serious damage wasn't the intention. On foggy Friday, when he really wanted to scare us, he had to make sure of his timing. That could explain Bowden Housteads in the wood. But for Monday's purpose, maybe he didn't have to get it perfect."

"So," Louise said, "what *was* his purpose?"

"More mischief, like burying the jammer in Cork's back garden. We shouldn't lose sight of the fact that he might have been playing with us again. In other words, he might've been trying to mislead us."

"And who'd want to mislead us?" Clare put in. "Someone who looked innocent after Monday's affair: our airport protesters – Vanessa and Ken – and Tim Darke."

"Exactly." Brett said, "I'm beginning to have my doubts about Tim Darke."

Clare replied, "Pity it's always the good-looking one."

Brett frowned. "Yeah. I noticed you thought that. And I noticed he..." Brett stopped. He was getting off the point.

With a grin, Clare said, "Only teasing. Anyway, what's bothering you – apart from that?"

"When we first asked him about air-band radio, he knew that the university wasn't lined up with the airport runway." Brett walked to the map and ran his finger along the line of the runway, extending it to Attercliffe and beyond, towards Hill Top. He stopped just north of the university campus. "See?

The campus isn't far off being in line. You'd only know it was down a bit if you'd studied a map. It was almost as if he'd considered it before we talked to him." Brett hesitated and then muttered, "And there's something else."

"What's that?" Clare enquired. "A motive?"

"I'm not sure…" He broke off and said, "Louise, get me a number for Naoki Matsumoto, will you?"

It didn't take long. It was still on file after they'd used the electronics professor in the Chapman case.

As soon as Brett got an answer, he said to the robotics expert, "When you first suggested that we speak to Tim Darke, you said he knew all about GPS. Why did you say that? Any particular reason?"

Naoki replied, "Yes, I suppose so. True, he knows all about GPS but he isn't its greatest admirer." The professor's kindly voice came out of Brett's earpiece and out of the loudspeakers in the incident room.

"Why's that?"

"It's a matter of professional pride. You see, Tim had his own ideas for a navigation system. He requested big funds to explore it. The research involved a clever modification to existing ground-based beacons. His application was turned down in favour of GPS."

"Thank you," Brett said. "That's why you said he hasn't been lucky with funding."

"What's it…?"

Interrupting, Brett commented, "I can't say just yet. But you've been very helpful, Naoki. Thanks again."

Brett turned to Clare and Louise. "There's your motive – and your grudge, Louise. Darke wants to discredit it because it sidelined his own research." Brett emphasised the word "sidelined". Then he added, "Maybe he didn't answer that localizer question in the quiz for fear of drawing attention to himself after all. And his office is crammed with old grey filing cabinets."

Clare said, "That would mean the dirt and fibres from the jammer are a real clue, Brett."

"And I dare say he uses the computers in his lab sometimes," Brett added. "If he's Strawberry, that could explain why we got a match with a single fibre from the fluff around Stefan's keyboard. Maybe it wasn't from Stefan but Tim Darke. Only one fragment because he doesn't use that computer much."

"What do you want to do?" asked Clare. "Go to his house, grab fibre samples, get his jeans to show to Greta and a photo to show to McPhee in case he's Mr Nash? He might've bought some components from the shop so they didn't all appear on the university's orders."

"Possibly," Brett responded. "As Stefan's supervisor, he could direct the research so Stefan had to buy quite a few of the necessary parts – just to pass the blame again."

"If Brendan Cork's not our man," Clare said, "Strawberry's tried to blame him as well. If we raided Tim's house, we could look for an air-band radio as well as another jammer. Strawberry must have had the radio to listen in to Kosler's transmissions about Brendan Cork. Otherwise, he wouldn't have known Cork was a suspect."

Brett sat down again. "It's a tricky decision, what to do. We're on the verge of a hand-over. *If* he's Strawberry, how's he going to react to us appearing on his doorstep tonight? If he thinks we're too close, he could call the whole thing off and just go hunting planes instead."

"It's a risk," Clare agreed. "Given what we know about him, I'd say it's a serious risk. He might even think it was fun."

"And it's not much good showing McPhee a photo of Tim Darke. If he's Nash, he was in disguise with glasses and moustache at least, so McPhee's not going to recognize him."

Louise chipped in, "I can check out his schooling, you know, but not till tomorrow morning. Thinking about it, I might not get anywhere till Monday morning when schools are open."

Clare added, "He's not going to leave incriminating evidence lying around so I doubt if we'd find electronic gear without turning his place upside down under a warrant. I suppose it's not a practical way forward when we've only got till tomorrow lunchtime before you begin your trot up the hill."

"OK," Brett said, making up his mind. "You're telling me we haven't got many viable options. We carry on with the marked money idea and double Darke's surveillance, especially between tomorrow afternoon and Monday morning."

"If he moves," Clare pointed out, "we can't mount a decent surveillance operation without radio or mobile phones. Without them, we couldn't co-ordinate all the cars and people we'd need for a pursuit. All we can do is watch and see if he leaves home. It's the same with the other suspects."

"That's all right. If he leaves, we let him go. The last thing we want to do is scare him off. He's got to pick up the ransom or my plan dies a death. We let Strawberry have a clear run at the money."

"That's hard," Clare said. "Like playing one of those kids' party games when you're supposed to cover your eyes and not peek. It's hard to turn your back on a million."

"You didn't cheat at those games, did you?"

"Well…"

Brett laughed. "Typical! Anyway, we can't afford to cheat tomorrow, Clare. Just to keep watch on the houses, we're going to have to be very careful."

"I know. But can we trust Kosler not to peek?"

"I hope so. I don't want him fouling it up again." Brett added, "In the meantime, there *is* something we can do. I'll see if I can get Naoki to slip into Darke's office tomorrow morning – as long as Tim isn't in residence. You never know what a friend might catch if he goes fishing with sticky tape for a hook."

"Like green fibres?"

"We can but hope."

*   *   *

As soon as Brett got close to sharing some intimate moments with Clare, the case shouldered them apart again. By the time that they finished work on Friday, the evening had gone. Instead they shared a pizza with Louise in the incident room and then went to their separate homes to sleep. It was going to be a trying weekend.

The teams out on surveillance duty reported from time to time by terrestrial telephone. As always, Dylan McPhee was serving in his busy shop. Danielle was at the airport. The last flight on a Saturday arrived at 14.15 so her watchers were assuming she'd be at work until about three o'clock. Vanessa and Ken were at work but Stefan had not left his digs. Brendan Cork was weeding his already immaculate garden. Michael Breach was at home, looking after the baby while his wife had gone out, carrying several bags. The officers guessed that she'd gone shopping. Unfortunately, Tim Darke had gone into work, foiling Brett's plan to take samples secretly from his office.

With the morning evaporating, Brett needed to head for Win Hill. He left Clare in charge of instructing Naoki when he could creep into Dr Darke's office with a roll of sticky tape. Besides, he needed Clare at headquarters to keep a responsible eye on Dennis Kosler.

Brett grasped the heavy suitcase and said, "Let's get on with it, then. We can't let Strawberry down. He's waiting for the biggest pay day of his life." He had selected Kosler's fittest-looking officer to accompany him. When Brett tired, he would need a lieutenant who could take over for a while. The sergeant, Pete, had a hobby of pot-holing so he was used to strenuous activity and wearing sturdy outdoor equipment.

"Good luck," Louise called.

"Thanks," he replied. "When I come back, my arms'll be ten centimetres longer."

"That'll improve your reach in the squash court," Clare said with a grin.

Stopping the windscreen wipers, Brett parked the four-wheel drive at the base of Win Hill, near the weir of Ladybower Reservoir. Together with the Thames Valley officer, he went to the rear of the jeep and got into his wet-weather walking gear. Before getting the suitcase, Brett asked, "Ready, Pete?"

Pete looked up to the summit way above them and muttered, "Say what you like about Strawberry, sir, he's got a terrific sense of humour."

Brett smiled. "You can't call me 'sir' all the way up. Brett'll do. I'll start with the money, you carry the spade and rope."

"All right. We'll take it in turns." Pete shook his head. "This is going to be the strangest hike of my life."

"Not me," Brett replied. "I always carry a suitcase of cash when I'm hiking in case I come across a pricey pub."

Brett had taken the precaution of wrapping the case completely in a plastic sheet. It kept out the rain and drizzle, protecting the liberal coating of invisible dye. Around the polythene he had attached straps and a comfortable handle. The suitcase could be carried normally or dragged by a longer grip. He had not used small wheels to convert it into a trolley-case because the terrain was too rough.

The shortest track to the summit was a steep and muddy path through the tangle of trees. Exposed tree roots should have supplied grip for their feet but, after the recent rainfall, the surface of the wood had become slimy and slippery. In places, crude steps had been cut into the hillside but erosion had made many of them useless. Often, Brett and Pete had to use branches and filthy roots to pull themselves up the steepest sections. They wedged the suitcase firmly against a trunk and clambered up to a secure position, the spade doubling as a helpful walking stick, and then hauled the case up with a rope attached to its straps. Sometimes, the path was virtually a stream and the two men splashed through it inelegantly.

During the exhausting walk, they took frequent breaks. They stood for a few minutes to get their breath back and to rest their tired arms and legs. Sometimes, they'd sit for a while on a fallen log but the wet and rotting wood was not exactly enticing.

Pete asked, "What if someone's up there and sees us burying the suitcase?"

"They'll dial 999 and ask for the police," Brett responded with a worn smile. "No, not in this miserable weather. It'll be deserted. No one's daft enough to climb up on a day like this. Except us." He looked upwards and added, "We'll be in low cloud soon – and out of the wood."

Nodding towards the suitcase, Pete said, "How do you think Strawberry's going to get it down again?"

"Relatively easily. My guess is he'll put the suitcase on some sort of board and let it slide down. It's slippery enough. He's only got to attach a rope to stop it getting out of control and running away from him. He might even take a longer, gentler path down. Or he may not want to be seen with this suitcase so he might leave it at the top and repack the cash into a couple of bags. I doubt if they'll have 'swag' written on them, though. Anyway, he obviously reckons it's worth all the problems to avoid cameras and surveillance. He's probably right."

Their trousers splattered with mud, they resumed their laborious ascent.

"It's crazy," Pete panted. "I'd have to work for fifty years in the Force to get this much money and here I am lugging it up a hill to leave it for a crook."

"I've climbed Ben Nevis a couple of times," Brett told him. "It's not particularly difficult but it goes on a bit. You always stop and have a chat with other hikers on the way up. I was told some soldiers once lugged a grand piano up to the summit and back."

"What on earth for?"

"Charity," Brett answered. "And because it hadn't been done before. It was a challenge." He heaved on the suitcase to lift it over a ditch. "That's how I feel right now."

They stopped talking to save their breath and to concentrate on negotiating another treacherously steep part of the woodland trail.

The slope eased when they emerged from the wooded area and on to grass and rock. It was much easier walking as they trudged towards the bare summit, directly in front of them. They couldn't see it, though. They were enveloped in mist. Behind them, the precipitous wood disappeared. "I needn't have worried about being seen," Pete murmured, still gasping for breath.

"Are you OK? Do you want a rest?" Brett asked as he carried the suitcase along the stony path, grateful for a good grip under his boots at last.

"No, I'm all right," Pete replied, deciding that to ask for a break would have been unmanly. Then he complimented Brett. "You're pretty fit."

"And rich – for the moment."

Using a position indicator, they located the patch of earth among the rocks, just to the east of the summit itself, where Strawberry had demanded that the ransom should be concealed. Following his orders, they dug a hole big enough to bury the suitcase. Brett removed the straps and slit the polythene jacket to expose the suitcase handle. From now on, anyone who touched it would be marked with the fluorescent tag. Brett manoeuvred the case into the hole and then they covered it with the scant turf. As instructed, they placed five large stones on top of the site, like flowers on a grave. Then they stood upright, stretched and took some deep breaths.

Just as Clare had predicted, it was hard to turn their backs on the treasure. "Will it be all right?" Pete asked.

Brett stepped back and examined their handiwork. "Don't worry. If you were a casual walker up here, would you notice anything strange?"

Pete surveyed the area. "No," he admitted.

"So, our little gold mine's perfectly safe," Brett said. "Besides, any visitors would be distracted by the beautiful scenery." He waved his arm towards the viewpoint where the panorama over Ladybower Reservoir should have been spectacular.

Pete laughed. In the cloud, he could hardly see the stone that marked the summit a few metres away.

"Still," Brett added, "at least it's not windy. It can be vicious up here."

"I'd rather go down holes," Pete replied. "The view's much the same and the wind's no problem."

Abandoning the fortune, they walked back down the track towards the wood. Going downhill without the heavy load, it seemed like an effortless stroll.

26

The incident room was on high alert, the atmosphere tense. As soon as Brett walked in, Clare took one look at him and turned up her nose. "You could have stopped off for a bath. You don't exactly look like a million dollars any more. Still, I suppose you want an update."

The team had discreetly positioned officers near every suspect but there would be no attempt to tail them if they moved. "McPhee's still in Electrics Unlimited," Clare reported. "Danielle's left the airport. She hasn't turned up at home yet, though. Michael Breach is another problem. He's gone out but we don't know where. Interesting that they're both whereabouts unknown. Anyway, our novelist's gone indoors, Vanessa and Ken are still on campus, and Stefan hasn't put his nose outside as far as we can tell. Tim Darke's gone home. And Wednesday are a goal down to Coventry. Tragic."

Brett refused to slump into a chair, even though his limbs ached for a break. "If Tim Darke's left his office, have we got some samples?"

Clare nodded. "Lots, courtesy of Naoki. I think he must have dragged a whole roll of sticky tape over every surface in the room. I've given them to Greta. She'd have e-mailed results by now except there were so many."

Brett smiled. "Good old Naoki." He paused and then checked, "Any more communication from Strawberry?"

"No," Louise answered. "Nothing."

"I wish we could get photos of Tim Darke's jeans," Brett muttered as he finally succumbed to the luxury of a chair and flexed the muscles in his sore arms.

"The men in a car outside his house volunteered to try," Clare told him. "I vetoed it. If they get close enough for taking fashion shots, they'd be too close. He might spot them and figure out we're on to him."

"Agreed," Brett replied. "It's a pity, but we can't risk it." Then he jumped up on his aching legs and said, "You stay here and oversee the operation, Clare. I'm off to the university."

The security chief looked him up and down suspiciously, grimaced, and checked Brett's warrant card again. Plainly, the man was trying to decide if this rough, muddy character really could be a detective inspector.

Brett explained, "I've just come in from a hike."

"Mmm." Still wary, he enquired, "What can I do for you?"

"You must have security cameras around most of the campus."

"Yes."

"How about one monitoring people coming and going from the Technology Faculty?"

On the huge array of television screens, the chief pointed at the screen labelled TF1. "That's the main door and reception by closed-circuit TV. TF2 covers the back door."

"Are there other entrances?"

"Yes, but we haven't got them covered."

"OK," Brett said. He was still optimistic. "I need as many video tapes from those two cameras as you've got."

"Oh? What for?"

Brett did not tell the whole truth in case the officer knew Dr Darke or turned uncooperative because Brett was investigating a fellow member of staff. "I have reason to believe a student or a visitor to the faculty in the last few days is a man we're looking for. He's not someone you want on your campus. If you've got him on video, I need to show his picture to an eye witness for identification."

"Do you have a warrant?"

"Look," Brett said, "I'll get one but, truth be told, I don't have time to apply to the magistrate. I'd prefer to have your co-operation. I assure you, you'd want me to get this character off your site. It's not trivial. In fact you'd say it's urgent. I'm talking a major crime – not one you want repeated on campus."

The security chief thought about it for a moment and then caved in. "OK. Just a minute. I'll get you what we've got, but make sure you return them as soon as you're done."

"Sure."

Eventually, the security guard produced a bundle of video tapes from the last three days. Taking the tapes in his arms, Brett asked, "You don't go back to a week last Friday, then?" He would have liked to have seen how Tim Darke was dressed on the afternoon that the plane crash-landed and Bowden Housteads was filmed coming out of the wood.

"No – or I'd be up to my neck in security tapes. We just keep a backlog of a few days."

"OK. Thanks."

Walking away from the security office, Brett felt only a little guilty for misleading the university. His need for a quick answer justified the fabrication. He'd rather lie now than have to explain to the press why hundreds of passengers had died near Heathrow.

Back at headquarters, Greta had communicated her staff's analysis of the unofficial samples from Dr Darke's office. Among the hairs, skin, dust, paper fragments, soil, there were plenty of fibres on Naoki's sticky tape. A few did match the green fibres found in the jammer. They were found among lots of orange fibres that had been identified as nylon and viscose rayon, commonly used for cushioned chairs. Forensics had deduced that the green polyester had come from the clothing of someone who had been seated in an orange chair.

"If the fibres are real evidence – not planted – it's looking grim for Tim Darke," Clare suggested.

"True," Brett said. "But, remember, it's not only Tim Darke who sits in his office. He'll have visitors and he'll probably have sessions with his research students in there."

As they spoke, phones were ringing at regular intervals as the various surveillance units reported in using cumbersome land-based telephones.

"Any sightings of Danielle and Michael Breach?" Brett enquired.

" 'Fraid not."

"Who knows what Tim Darke looks like?" Brett called out.

Nobody responded. Only the officers who'd been assigned to him could identify him and they were sitting in a car outside his house.

It was up to Brett and Clare to trawl tediously through the video tapes, looking for images of Tim Darke in case he had been captured in jeans. "While we're watching telly, Louise, can you sort out a way of scanning images into the computer so we can pass a digital version electronically to Greta. That way, she can analyze them for jean wear-patterns straight-away. Then we can have an answer in minutes." To

Clare, he said, "I'll start with this morning's tapes. You do Friday's. Concentrate on the morning arrivals and people leaving in the evening. For speed, we'll ignore the rest of the day – at least at first."

Brett and Clare were half an hour into the tapes, playing them at double speed, when Brett commented, "There's only a limited amount of fun you can get out of looking at a picture of a front door and the occasional person coming through it, isn't there?"

"Let's hope we're not wasting our time, looking at the wrong doors," Clare replied without shifting her eyes from the screen. "Perhaps he uses a side door."

"Not always," Brett said, suddenly coming to life. "Louise! Images to copy to Forensics." The screen showed Tim Darke coming into work at 9.32 that morning. He was wearing a pair of dark jeans. Using slow motion, Brett went through the video pictures with Tim in shot until he found the image that gave the clearest impression of his jeans. "There," he said to Louise. "That's the one to transmit."

While Louise arranged it, Clare carried on with the boring job, checking Friday's security tapes, and Brett consulted Kosler. But there was no further action to report from suspect surveillance. Brett returned to the video and inserted the first of Thursday's tapes.

By the time that Clare hit the jackpot, Greta had e-mailed back her summary. *Image of Dr Darke at work today versus individual termed Bowden*

Housteads: no match. The quality of the image of Darke's jeans is poor (too distant) but sufficient to prove negative within 95 per cent confidence. In a second disappointment, Clare's find was unhelpful. Yesterday, Tim Darke had worn light-coloured trousers. Without delay Clare switched to Wednesday's closed-circuit TV tapes.

Three quarters of an hour later, Kosler shouted, "We've got movement."

But it wasn't Tim Darke.

"Rzepinski's just got on a bus. Stan's checked it out on local timetables. It goes to Bamford village. According to the map, that's within easy walking distance of Win Hill."

"A bus?" Brett exclaimed. "What was he wearing?"

"Boots, jeans and kagool."

"Was he carrying anything?" Brett asked.

"A rucksack and what looked like two empty holdalls," Kosler answered.

Brett exchanged a glance with Pete. "He's not going to take a million pounds home on a bus, is he?" Brett murmured.

"Could be," Clare said. "Let's face it, he looks like a lost visitor to the country. He could pull it off. He'd look like a hundred other bedraggled tourists, carting his stuff around in bulging bags, using the cheapest form of transport he can find. He won't look out of place once he's down the hill and back on the main road. He might even hitch a lift back."

"Good point. You're right. I like the idea of

hitching around with a million quid stuffed in bags," Brett replied.

"If it was December, he'd probably blend in by using a bushy beard, red tunic and huge sack."

Brett smiled and nodded but then turned serious. "If only we could tail him."

"It's all right," Kosler put in. "I've positioned some men in Bamford and the wooded part of the hill."

"You've done what?" Brett cried.

"They're fully kitted out as hikers. Very convincing."

Brett groaned aloud. "They'd better be." He could not bring Kosler's men back without breaking radio silence. He muttered, "They're not wired, are they? You know Strawberry made their ears bleed last time."

"I'm no fool, Brett."

"What are their orders?" Brett snapped at his troublesome colleague.

"Just to watch."

"Not to arrest?"

"No. At least, not till I ... we give the order."

Brett sighed. "You couldn't turn your back on that much money, could you?"

Kosler retorted, "I'm saving your skin, Inspector Lawless. If it was left to you, we'd never see that money again. You'll thank me when this is over."

"You've lost sight of what's important here," Brett said angrily. "The million's just a means to an end. What matters is keeping planes safely up in the air."

At least Kosler's men were maintaining radio silence. If Strawberry was listening to the airwaves, he would not discover what they were doing. The officers in the incident room relied on infrequent terrestrial telephone calls to update them. Apparently, Stefan got off the bus in the village and headed straight for Win Hill. He was said to be looking nervous and shifty.

All of a sudden, the heat had gone out of the search through the university's security tapes for pictures of Tim Darke's jeans. Instead, the real action seemed to be happening on Win Hill. Brett and Clare stuck close to Kosler. They hoped to stop the Thames Valley officer springing any more nasty surprises but they were painfully aware that he could claim that this was his extortion case and that he held a superior rank. Together, the tense squad waited impatiently for Stefan to come down from Win Hill.

Actually, the research student got to the peak and back quite quickly but it seemed like for ever. From the public telephone box, one of Kosler's team informed his boss that Stefan had just walked wearily into the village.

"Can you see him?" Dennis flicked the switch to divert the responses to the loudspeaker so everyone could hear.

"Yes. He's heavily loaded with bags – one in each hand. And ... he's gone straight past the bus stop. He's put his bags down, resting maybe. No, he's looking up and down the road. Is he waiting for a lift? I don't know."

"Sounds promising," Kosler replied. "Give the signal to Murphy."

Interrupting, Brett said, "Hang on. What signal? Who's Murphy?"

Dennis put his hand over the mouthpiece. "My best man. It's a little idea I came up with. Me and Stan. Sit back and see what you can do with a good computer man."

Joyfully, the officer in the phone box said, "Subject's swallowed the bait. He's got into the taxi. Hey. He's turning round, going north. He's not going back to Sheffield the same way."

"OK," Kosler replied. "I've got it covered."

"You'd better explain this," Brett muttered warily.

"I put Murphy in a taxi. Not a real taxi. It's paid

off, as it happens."

"I bet you've attached a transmitter to it. Where is it? Underneath?"

"Keep calm. There's no sign Rzepinski's carrying electronic gear. He won't detect it."

Stan shouted, "He's turned right on to the A57, heading back into Sheffield the other way." A flashing dot decorated the map on Stan's monitor.

Kosler's eyes also flashed. "Good, eh? No need for your chemical tagging after all."

Brett was not sure what to think. He wanted to give Kosler the benefit of the doubt. He did not condemn his tactics outright. His plan might just work. But he had a horrible feeling that it was too easy. Brett could not see Strawberry falling into a conventional trap. He waited for something to go wrong.

Stan reported, "He's turned left off the A57. He's taken a tiny road at Hollow Meadows."

Dennis, Brett and Clare all realized at the same time. The road led to Hill Top. "He's going to Cork's place!"

"Right," Kosler said. "I'm taking over. This isn't attempted murder at an airport. It's heavy-duty blackmail and what did John Macfarlane say? It's my baby. We play to my rules from now on." Breaking radio silence, he yelled, "All units – I mean, *all* surveillance units – to Hill Top. I've seen enough. We're moving in."

Brett and Clare could only stare at each other.

"So, I was right," Kosler uttered. "Cork's our man.

And I always suspected a double act with Rzepinski."

"You might be right," Brett admitted. "The green fibres on Tim Darke's chair could easily have come from Stefan. But," he added, "it doesn't explain Bowden Housteads."

"No," Dennis replied abruptly. "I say he's got nothing to do with it. You've been indulging in wishful thinking because you came up with this jeans-fingerprinting idea that you thought would make you famous." He came very close to sniggering.

"And what about Mr Nash?"

"Another red herring."

Brett glanced at Strawberry's wall chart. "What about the clash with a science teacher?"

"You've blown it, Brett. Look at Stan's screen. All the evidence you could ask for is right there in front of you: Rzepinski heading for Cork's house with the money. What else do you need? And how do you explain what's happening if it's not a Rzepinski/Cork double act?"

Brett sighed. "I don't know but I'm still uneasy about it."

"Well, I don't care," Dennis responded. "You stand around and be uneasy while I get on and wrap it up. All cars are homing in on Hill Top – along with Rzepinski and the money. It won't be long now."

Brett looked at Clare to gauge her feelings.

Speaking quietly and privately to her partner, she said, "We know it's dangerous to go for a complicated answer when a simple one's staring us in the face. It looks clear-cut but ... I'm with you, Brett. Strawberry's too sharp for this. It'd suit his sense of fun if all this was a wild–goose chase. But how could he – or she – arrange it?" She shook her head.

A spooky voice echoed round the incident room, "Closing in on Hill Top, sir. All roads covered. They'll be surrounded."

Brett murmured, "There's got to be a sting in the tail."

"I guess we'll find out any minute now."

But everything went smoothly, as Kosler's satisfied expression indicated. As soon as Brendan Cork opened his front door and Stefan held out the heavy holdalls, the Thames Valley team closed in on them from every direction. It was a swift and efficient operation, taking the two men by complete surprise. There were no weapons, no scuffles, no violence. Rzepinski and Cork were cuffed before they could put up any resistance.

The detached voice reported, "We're all secure here, sir. Both subjects under arrest. But, you know the money?"

Kosler's smug expression suddenly changed. "Of course I do. What about it?"

"It's gone, sir."

"It's what?"

"Rzepinski's bags are full of A4 papers. That's what he was delivering. They're manuscripts of some sort."

"What?" Kosler cried again.

"He's not got…"

"I heard," Kosler barked. "Damn! Well, don't just stand there. Ask him where the money is."

The radio went silent for a few minutes. Dennis wasn't quiet, though. He stomped up and down the incident room, mumbling to himself. Once, he glanced at Brett with a scowl on his face. Perhaps he expected Brett to be relishing his discomfort.

Brett wasn't relishing anything. He feared a twist rather than hoped for it. He was just as concerned and surprised as Kosler. He might have anticipated a problem, but not this one.

The distant voice crackled into life. "Rzepinski says he got the money and hid it somewhere else on the hill but he's not saying where."

"It doesn't make sense. Why did he do that?" Kosler demanded to know.

"He's not saying that either."

Dennis shook his head in exasperation. "What a mess! Bring them both in. Make it fast. We've got some sorting out to do."

Louise was not paying attention to the frayed nerves that had developed into elation and then collapsed to bewilderment and anger. She was getting on calmly with some work. She called quietly, "Brett! Clare!" In the excitement of the arrest, they had forgotten her. While they were preoccupied with Stefan Rzepinski, she'd studied the image of Dr Darke that Brett had found and then searched for the same person on some of the remaining tapes. Using her initiative, she'd piped to Greta the best picture that she'd found from one of Wednesday's tapes. "I hope you don't think I'm…"

"I think you're fantastic," Brett said.

"So do I," Clare added. "What's the answer?"

Louise hit the return button on her keyboard and let them read Greta's message for themselves.

Image of Dr Darke at work on Wednesday 10th September versus individual termed Bowden Housteads: probable match. The quality of the photograph of Darke's jeans is poor (too distant) but sufficient to suggest positive match with 85 per cent confidence.

Brett put his hand on her shoulder. "I think you just got yourself a permanent posting with us – if you want it."

Beaming, Louise looked up at him and nodded. From somewhere inside her, she plucked up the courage to be playful for once. "You know, I can think of worse things."

"Do we go and see Dr Darke, then?" Clare asked Brett.

"Let's wait to see what Stefan and Brendan Cork say first," Brett answered. "You see, I still have faith in the tag."

Clare smiled. "Still not taking a sneaky peek in that kids' game?"

"Unlike some," he replied with a grin, "I never cheated."

"Yeah. Sure."

"Well, I never got caught."

Kosler had his two suspects installed separately in two different interview rooms. Cork, though, was like a rock. He denied knowing the young man who had turned up on his doorstep and offered him some weighty bags. He denied knowing what was in the holdalls. He denied having anything to do with threats to aircraft. He denied everything strenuously.

As a spectator, Clare witnessed Brendan's performance. Afterwards, she whispered to Brett, "Cork's got the outrage of someone falsely accused."

"Mmm. Interesting."

"Fancy gatecrashing Interview Room 2 and taking a look at Kosler trying his luck with Rzepinski?" asked Clare.

"Good idea," Brett replied. "Just let me get something first."

When they entered, Kosler's sidekick said, "DI Lawless and DS Tilley have entered the interview room." He spoke for the benefit of the rolling cassette recorder.

Stefan looked harassed. Kosler was pacing up and down while his sergeant glared at the student from very close quarters.

"So," Dennis growled, "you're saying you were doing a favour for a Polish friend who might or might not have connections with some dodgy Polish outfit. This friend sent you an e-mail, telling you, for the good of Poland or something, to go up Win Hill, collect a suitcase full of money from one spot, hide it somewhere else where you'd find some manuscripts. Then you were to take them to a mystery address in Hill Top."

"Yes."

"You claim you don't know who lived there."

"That is right."

Kosler stopped by the table and banged his fist down on it. "Where did you put the money?"

Stefan said nothing. He just shook his bowed head.

"Where?"

"I am not to say." Stefan looked up in distress. "I am digging up the bag with the money and putting it somewhere else in the wood. That is all I say."

"And you've said it over and over again. Now tell me *really* why you did it."

"Because I follow instructions."

Brett and Clare watched silently as he was mentally pummelled by Kosler. "Is he lying about re-burying the cash?" Brett asked Clare in a whisper.

"I reckon so."

Brett stepped forward and, not looking at Dennis, said, "Just two questions, Stefan. What colour was the suitcase with the money?"

Stefan sniffed loudly. "I don't know. I am not remembering."

"OK. Put your hands out on the table."

"What?"

"Just do it please." Brett watched the student offer his hands hesitantly. "No. Palms up, please. That's right." Brett told the officer by the door to turn off the lights, then he shone the ultraviolet lamp on to Stefan's upturned palms. The whites of the student's shirt cuffs shone brilliantly but his hands remained shadowy in the darkness. Not a trace of spectral blue. "Thank you," Brett said.

"What is this being about?" Stefan asked as the light went back on, revealing his puzzled frown.

"Second question, Stefan. You went to a weekend conference at Middlesex University. Did Tim Darke go as well?"

"Yes."

"Thanks. That's all I need for now."

Stefan looked surprised.

"Along with some other facts," Brett told him, "that might be enough to get you out of this mess. When I come back, you might even feel able to tell me why you're lying about the money."

Without another word, Brett and Clare left the room. But Kosler, appearing in the corridor behind them, shouted, "What was that about?"

"It's not Rzepinski and Cork," Brett replied. "They're clean. So clean they're spotless."

"Yeah," Dennis shouted with extreme sarcasm. "Like leopards. With acne."

Brett and Clare walked away. They would get on with the case while Kosler pursued his theory obstinately, obsessively and ineffectually.

28

Clare sighed. "I wish Kosler hadn't jumped in at the deep end and withdrawn all the surveillance. Now we don't know when the real Strawberry's gone up Win Hill. We don't know when to try the blue-hand test."

"Soon," Brett suggested. "I bet Strawberry's plotted all this. In his grand design, he anticipated us sending everyone to Hill Top, leaving the way clear for him to retrieve the ransom. I wouldn't be surprised if he's getting it now. It'll be dark soon so he can use the cover. Let him. I don't want to go back up Win Hill myself to get it. I'm too tired. We'll let Strawberry do the hard labour then nab him – and his jammer – afterwards."

"Stefan didn't handle the suitcase at all, did he? He's just been told to tell us that. Really, he went up

the hill for the papers that Strawberry planted somewhere. That's all."

"Exactly."

They took a quick look at Stefan's haul. It
consisted of downloaded Internet web pages. They
seemed to be a cocktail of activists' literature. Animal
rights campaigners, environmental groups, right-
wing political tracts, left-wing political tracts, the
anti-abortion lobby, groups opposed to genetic
experiments, Polish dissidents. It was an unfocused
ragbag of protest literature.

"Let's give it all to Greta," Brett said.

Clare looked at the extent of it and replied, "Yeah,
she'll be delighted."

"There must be plenty of trace evidence in there
somewhere. Hairs, skin, fibres. Lots."

"Do we need them?" Clare queried. "We're saying
Tim Darke's Strawberry. He's the one with enough
knowledge of Stefan to sew him up. All it needed was
a faked e-mail from a friend and poor old gullible
Stefan thought he was the James Bond of Poland,
delivering dodgy anti-establishment literature and
providing a diversion."

"Strawberry's pretty shrewd. If we're going to nail
him, we'll need as much evidence as we can get.
Bowden Housteads, the jeans, some green fibres and
an old filing cabinet aren't enough."

"What do we do?"

Brett answered, "Give him his triumph tonight. Let
him think we're barking up the wrong tree. Tomorrow

we hunt the crook with the glowing hands."

"And a million quid, don't forget."

"Easily overlooked," Brett said with a grin, "but I'll try to bear it in mind while we do the crucial job."

"Stopping him sabotaging more planes."

"Exactly."

"And we start with Tim Darke?" asked Clare.

"We sure do."

Coming up behind them, Big John said, "I suggest you change your minds. What if Strawberry decides to do a runner as soon as he gets his hands on the ransom? What if he leaves the country? I need that money back, Brett. It's not expendable. The night's still young for police officers."

"But we don't know for sure if he's collected…" Brett looked into John's determined face and stopped talking. "Yes, sir. OK."

"That's better," John muttered as he turned and walked back to his office.

Clare said to her partner, "This is going to test your stamina, isn't it? Up the hill again to see if the money's gone, then search for the blue blackmailer, all before bedtime."

"I could send Louise with you."

"And miss out? You wouldn't dream of it."

"Come on," he said. "Let's get togged up and find some good torches."

Clare laughed. "It's going to look like an episode of the X-Files."

* * *

The moon was smeared by a thick layer of cloud. Win Hill was a prominent and forbidding black mass. Clare peered at it through the windscreen and said to her partner, "It's steep and high. You must be knackered already."

"I'm not in peak condition, no."

"OK," she said with a grin. "Let's have a race. Last one to the summit buys the beers."

"I might as well cough up now."

"Look on the bright side," Clare said to him. "While Strawberry's mind's on retrieving the money at least he's not tinkering about with his GPS jammer. He's not killing people at Heathrow and Gatwick."

She parked at the edge of Bamford village and they walked the rest of the way. They didn't drive right to the base of the hill because their approaching car would be very easy to spot in the narrow deserted lanes. If Strawberry was still in the area, their headlights and engine noise might make him nervous.

"Before we trot up the hill," Clare whispered, "let's look around and see if there's a car parked in any of the obvious places. It'd save us a lot of effort and bother if we can just wait by Strawberry's car."

"True, but would you expect Strawberry to leave his car somewhere obvious with a big sign on it, saying *Gone to get the loot?*"

"Probably not," Clare replied, "but he thinks the heat's off. He thinks we're still trying to crack Brendan Cork and make sense of Stefan Rzepinski's story."

Padding quietly along the track at the bottom of the hill and peering behind the first line of trees, they did not spot any parked cars. Instead they headed for the woodland trail and began their torchlight ascent. Both of them held their torches with a forefinger hovering over the on/off button. The beams made two claustrophobic tunnels through the dark wood. For an instant, the trunks of silver birches caught in the rays really looked like silver. Confused by the unexpected shafts of light, insects glistened brightly like a fluorescent dye under an ultraviolet lamp.

The wood smelled damp and musty. Uncannily, the darkness seemed to amplify every sound. Somewhere a fox barked. Nearer, the trickling water of a stream sounded like a torrent. The detectives' footfalls boomed, every twig that they snapped sounded like a pistol firing, every step in a muddy pool was a loud splash. The rustling and pattering of the wood's night-time occupants became a covert stampede. Overhead, the fluttering of bats and birds seemed more sinister than natural and harmless.

At a bank, Clare scrambled up first. Just as she was hauling herself up acrobatically, there was a sudden screech. "What was that?" Brett breathed, alarmed by the intense shriek.

"An owl," Clare replied. "To be precise, a little owl, I think."

Brett exhaled. "They should stick to traditional, friendly hooting."

At the top of the bank, Clare hooked her arm

round a sturdy branch, her torch dangling from her fingers, and reached down with her free hand. "Here," she said in a hush.

Brett grabbed her hand and heaved himself up a vertical face of mud and greasy roots. Joining her, he said, "It's a bit easier without a heavy suitcase." He looked ahead but did not shine his torch into the distance. "My turn to go first?"

"After you," Clare replied.

Brett put out a hand to grab a branch but abruptly withdrew it. He put one finger to his lips and, with the other, killed his torchlight. Immediately, Clare did the same. They stood to attention, still and silent. Along with the constant gurgling of water and occasional scrabbling of small animals, there was another noise. It was the slapping down of heavy boots and a low uneven scraping. It came from somewhere above them and to the right. Someone was striding down a parallel path. Brett pointed towards the source of the noise. Just able to make out his partner, Brett saw her nod. Neither of them could pick out the beam of a torch but the sound was unmistakable. Someone was coming downhill and dragging something or, more likely, holding it back so it didn't get out of control.

Clare stepped lightly towards Brett and whispered into his ear. "Well? Do we take him here?"

Brett answered, "Not if it was up to me. I don't care about the money. I'd let him go but John would eat us alive if we missed a chance to reclaim his lottery cash."

Clare nodded. "Follow till we're on easier ground?"

"He'll hear us or see our lights."

"There's no hope of creeping up on him quietly – even with torches on so we can see where we're going."

"Agreed. We're just going to have to rush him."

Thinking back to their case in the Caribbean, Clare murmured, "Chasing people through woods is getting to be a habit."

The distant rumble and squelching footfalls stopped. Strawberry was taking a breather, or he had heard them and he was listening, or he had come to a sheer drop and was figuring out how to tackle it. Brett and Clare stopped whispering and remained motionless. The nocturnal noises of the wood covered up their shallow breathing. The stand-off lasted three long minutes. Then the unseen walker in the wood resumed his descent.

Brett and Clare looked at each other. "Just go for it?" Clare queried quietly.

Brett nodded. "And hope at least one of us makes it."

They waited until they could see a dancing shaft of torchlight, sliced by intervening tree trunks, about fifty metres away. Then, simultaneously, they switched on their own torches and crashed clumsily into the undergrowth in the direction of the shrouded walker.

Now he was really annoyed. Immediately he knew what had happened. Dennis Kosler had fallen for it, lock, stock and barrel, but not that Inspector Lawless. As soon as Strawberry heard the commotion on the main path, as soon as he saw two unstable beams heading in his direction, he knew. He didn't need daylight to recognize Lawless and Tilley. They were the only ones who were capable of seeing through his scam. He cursed in anger – and, at the same time, admired. But he also knew what to do. The money was unimportant now. He had the power – the weapon – to double, treble, quadruple the stakes later. The important thing was to get away. He was certain that Lawless and Tilley had no idea who he was. They knew only who he wasn't.

No, the important thing was not being identified.

He was convinced that he hadn't left behind any telltale clues. He'd been very careful. He'd cleaned the first jammer so there couldn't be much left inside. On that foggy day, he'd taken a taxi to Bowden Housteads Wood, not given a name, and worn a disguise. On Monday, he'd set up the jammer in his own home on a timer switch once he'd learned by phone that Flight UK2185 was on time. He'd got the components for his jammers from all over the place. The Internet, the university's electronics department, Electrics Unlimited. In the Attercliffe shop, he had used another disguise and a false name. No, he hadn't left any clues. Lawless was floundering in the dark, just like he would on Win Hill.

In another way, Strawberry was glad. DI Lawless was giving him the perfect excuse to carry on jamming GPS signals. If GPS wasn't already compromised beyond salvation, it soon would be. No doubt at all. Strawberry would go to Heathrow with glee now, intent on destroying the aircraft system for ever. The authorities would pay a very high price before he'd finished playing with their toys like a careless, impatient, impetuous child. In a temper, he'd toss them down, smashing them to pieces. All courtesy of Detective Inspector Brett Lawless.

Strawberry knew the Win Hill terrain. That was one reason he'd chosen it. He tipped the suitcase from his sledge, wiped its handle to obliterate any fingerprints and, unencumbered, strode down the ill-formed path. It was a gentler, easier way than the one marked on the map, and the detectives attempting to cross between the two would soon be entangled in undergrowth, bogged down in a brook, unable to contend with the slope. He'd be away in his concealed car while they were still homing in on their precious cash.

Tonight, before these detectives knocked on the doors of all their suspects, he would be home, relaxed, in changed clothes, with clean walking boots, sledge washed and put away. They might not even regard him as a suspect. He might not get a visit from them at all but, just in case, he'd be prepared.

He was beginning to see all sorts of reasons to smile while he loped as quickly as possible down the trail.

Strawberry had eluded them. His bobbing light had long since disappeared from view. The ground that Brett and Clare had tried to cover was so rough that they couldn't keep their eyes on Strawberry's beam and their feet on the ground at the same time. It was a hopeless one-sided chase. They heard the roar of a car's engine just when they found the abandoned suitcase.

Squatting down by it, Clare said despondently, "Do you reckon he touched the tagged parts at all? He could've manhandled the whole thing, only touching the plastic."

"No," Brett answered. "I bet he dragged it out the hole by the handle and he'll have opened it up to check what was inside before he humped it all the way down the hill. He'll have touched the right bits."

Brett flicked open the lid to reveal a staggering number of notes by torch light.

Clare murmured, "Big John's money found safe and sound, insurers happy, and Strawberry away with invisible stains on his hands, but no arrest."

"It could've been a lot worse," Brett said. "At least we didn't even have to go far up the hill."

"We didn't confiscate the jammer either."

"No," Brett said. "I'm afraid not. That's why we don't take the money straight back to HQ. First stop's got to be Darke's place. If he's Strawberry, we catch him cold – before he has a chance to attack any more air traffic."

Clare nodded in agreement. "Yeah. His blood might be up now. Let's get going." Trying to put the bleak thought to the back of her mind, she added, "If someone nicks the car tonight, they'll get a very pleasant surprise when they open the boot. Anyway, I'll let you carry the cash back into Bamford. After all, you're experienced at it."

"Thanks." Taking a deep breath, Brett said, "I'm going to ruin any fingerprint evidence by doing this but I suppose that's the penalty for making the money safe." He picked up the suitcase and headed towards the orange glow of streetlights over Bamford.

Tim Darke was dressed in spotless black trousers and a green sweatshirt bearing the logo of the Massachusetts Institute of Technology. He looked calm and settled for the evening.

"We're not disturbing you?" Brett began.

"No," Tim answered. "Come in. I was just watching Match of the Day. If you know the scores, don't tell me. Surely Wednesday can slaughter Coventry?"

In the living room, Brett sat down but Clare remained standing by the door.

"What can I do for you this time?" Tim asked pleasantly, turning down the volume of the fervent football commentary.

"It's back to GPS and navigation in general," Brett said. "You must have been cut up about having your own ideas turned down in favour of GPS."

Unruffled, Dr Darke replied, "Oh, you know about that. Yes, I wanted to research another way forward – less prone to interference – but the powers-that-be went down the GPS route. I wasn't delighted but, in academic life, you apply for lots of research grants. The going rate is one success out of every four. You can't get too upset by rejections when it happens 75 per cent of the time."

Thinking back to Strawberry's first demand, Brett asked, "How much money did you apply for? Half a million?"

Tim looked surprised. "I don't remember the exact amount but it'd be about that."

Brett nodded. "Have you got walking boots?"

"Funny question," Tim noted. "But, yes, I have."

"Can I see them, please?"

He looked puzzled but said, "I suppose so." He rose from his seat and left the room.

Clare frowned. If he was innocent, she believed that he would have objected more or queried the request. Unless he was very laid back.

When he returned, he smiled at Clare as he walked past her. He handed the boots to Brett. "There you are. Even if I don't know why you want them."

"Nice pair," Brett observed. "And very clean. In fact, still wet."

"Correct. I went out in them this afternoon," Tim explained. "It was a choice between supermarket shopping or fresh air in the Peaks. Guess which I went for."

"I can understand that," Brett replied as he put them down by the side of the chair. "Where were you Saturday 30th August to Monday 1st September?"

"Er... That was a London conference. I went down south with my research students."

"Have you got a timer?"

"A timer?" Darke repeated. "What do you mean?"

"A mains timer so you can record Match of the Day when you're not here."

"Yes. I've got two or three. Useful things. Why?"

Brett had no intention of answering any questions himself. He was darting from topic to topic, trying to confuse the lecturer. "Do you know a man called Nash?"

"Nash? Yes. There are two Nashes at the university. Are you thinking of one particular Nash?"

"Never mind."

Clare watched Tim carefully. He was very cool

under fire. Or he was nothing to do with Nash and Strawberry. She could easily believe that he was telling the truth. She could easily believe that they were chasing the wrong man. Brett was going to have to resort to heavy tactics soon if he was going to prove that Tim Darke, Nash, Strawberry and Bowden Housteads were all the same person.

"What type of school did you go to?"

"For my sins, my parents sent me to an independent."

"How did you get on? Were you always into physics?"

"Just about. But I was the classic underachiever, I'm afraid. I was too restless, bored with the curriculum." He paused before adding, "I wanted the big bang and black holes but I got forces on billiard balls."

"So, you had a stormy time with the staff?"

Tim smiled. "As I recall, we had a few chats about concentration and the need to pass exams and coursework. But I did anyway. I did just enough to get to university and on to those big juicy ideas."

"Where were you on Friday the fifth?" Brett asked.

"At work."

"Strange," Brett replied. "We've got you coming out of Bowden Housteads Wood that afternoon."

"Bowden Housteads Wood?" He shook his head. "I think you've got a case of mistaken identity there. I was at the university, slaving over hot lecture notes."

Clare noted that he didn't question the evidence. She expected him to ask Brett what linked him to the edge of the wood. After all, scientists were famed for their curiosity. Either he regarded Brett's statement as too ridiculous to question, or he wanted to drop the subject as quickly as possible.

Brett asked, "On the quiz night, did you not answer the localizer question because your mind was on something else? Perhaps on something you'd set up with a mains timer?"

"I don't know what you're talking about, I'm afraid. I told you why I didn't answer. A bit of cheating was going on. And there were Sergeant Tilley's lightning reactions." He glanced up at her, seeking a friendly face amid Brett's hostile inquisition.

"All right," Brett said, finally admitting to himself that he needed a sturdier battering ram against such a brick wall. "I want to show you something."

"Oh?"

Brett looked towards Clare and nodded at the light switch. Suddenly, the room was lit only by the television screen. The wallpaper and ceiling reflected vividly changing colours but mainly the green of the football pitch. Tim's face flickered as if he were sitting by a fire in a cave. Extracting the handheld UV lamp from his jacket pocket, Brett said, "Tonight I picked up a suitcase from a wood. I can prove it because, when I touched it, I transferred a fluorescent dye from it on to my hand. See?" He turned on the lamp and his right hand became a second source of light in the room. It glowed bright blue in the gloom.

Tim looked at the detective's ghostly hand and then stared into his eyes which seemed to shift with the ebb and flow of the football match.

Then, suddenly, Tim jumped out of his seat and dashed for the door.

Lunging, Brett was not fast enough to grab him.

By the glimmer from the television, Clare stepped into the doorway. She was not even distracted by the Sky Blues' goal.

Darke ran at her full tilt, shoulder first. He expected to barge her out of the way. But he didn't even manage to touch her. She side-stepped and, in the same movement, brought up her left leg, flooring him immediately. Before he could respond, her knee was pressing into the small of his back and she had clasped both of his hands tightly behind him.

Cuffing the winded lecturer, Brett said, "You forgot Sergeant Tilley's lightning reactions." While Clare continued to hold Tim down, Brett turned on the ultraviolet light above the locked hands. At once, they both blazed blue.

After Brett had cautioned Dr Darke, Clare said, "I don't think you're going to see any more of the match so I'll tell you now. They lost 2-1."

31

The sweatshirt that Tim had been wearing when he was arrested was made from the same type of fibre that had been found in the first jammer. A thorough combing of Tim's house revealed the jeans that matched the pair worn by Bowden Housteads. It also turned up an air-band radio tuned to police frequencies. At Dr Darke's office, the police team found the second jammer locked in a grey filing cabinet. In the same drawer, there was a deep red executive attaché case with combination locks. And one of the precision screwdrivers in his laboratory had a microscopic stain of white primer and beige topcoat. At last, Strawberry had been exposed.

Eventually, Greta's staff found a hair among the piles of papers delivered to Brendan Cork. The DNA in the root matched Tim Darke's and the case against the lecturer was complete.

After the arrest, Clare explained to Stefan how he had been duped. Then the embarrassed student opened up. He had been fooled into thinking that he was doing a favour for a cult in Poland by becoming a decoy. Darke's e-mail message telling Stefan what to do on Win Hill seemed to have come from a fellow cult member. It informed Stefan that his actions would distract the police while a friend picked up the real prize from the hill: money destined for the Polish group. The note also instructed Stefan to tell the police that he'd moved the money.

Brett and Clare understood at once why Darke had told Stefan to lie. If the student had not convinced Kosler that he'd shifted the money to a secret location, Kosler would have sent a team to keep watch on the burial site at the summit. That would have scuppered Tim's plan.

Stefan Rzepinski's worst crime was his blind faith in e-mail messages. Brett and Clare released the lonely student without charge.

Brett also freed an indignant Brendan Cork. "Look on it like this," Brett said to the writer. "We've given you lots of opportunity to see life in a police station from the bad guys' perspective. It'll be useful for your follow-up novel."

"I might just do that. A story about wrongful arrest, police brutality, the full works."

"Hardly brutal," Brett replied. "Anyway, just make sure you change all the names."

* * *

The job done, most of Kosler's team set out for home territory on Sunday. Before driving south, Pete raised a sober can of Pepsi to Brett and said, "Any time you want to get into pot-holes, just call. You'd love it and I'd be happy to show you the ropes."

"Thanks. I'll bear it in mind. But rock formations above ground are more my style."

On Monday, when DS Kosler had convinced himself that they'd got Tim Darke wrapped up, the Thames Valley chief also decided to leave. The final debriefing was more of a parting than a party. If it could be called a festive occasion, it was because Brett and Clare used it to celebrate Kosler's departure as much as the closing of the case.

Getting as close as he would ever get to congratulating Brett, Dennis muttered, "You got lucky with those jeans."

Not allowing Brett to respond, John Macfarlane put in, "Yes, he did. But that's not half the story. Some officers wouldn't know luck if it beat them about the head and body. Brett and Clare are seriously good at recognizing and using it."

"Mmm." Dennis would not argue with a superior but that did not mean he would openly agree.

Brett said, "Maybe we wouldn't have cracked it if it hadn't been for Louise carrying on the video work while we were getting carried away with Rzepinski." He wanted to acknowledge Louise's part and to hear Kosler admit that he was wrong about her.

"Mmm." Dennis put down his glass and said,

"Still, I can't stay here nattering. Some of us have got important police work to do, see?"

"You know," Clare pronounced, "you do make a genius veggie curry." In the semi-darkness, she took a drink of deep red wine. Looking round the room that shimmered uncannily by the light of Brett's aquarium, she said, "It's like the glow of a black-mailer's hands in here."

Brett grinned. "You're avoiding the issue."

"All right," she replied. "This is the choice. We're a partnership in crime or a couple, but not both at the same time. We came down on the side of crime but now you're wanting a rethink."

Brett nodded. "Don't you as well?"

"I've got a load of hungry friends hanging on my every word, eager to form a queue for you."

"Clare, I'm not interested in them. I'm only…"

She looked at him and, not entirely seriously, said, "If you're voting for us being a couple, you're really saying you could do without me at work."

"No, of course I'm not. You know I think you're a terrific partner. I can't imagine doing the job without you now. I don't even know I'd be any good at it without you. But…"

"Yes?" Clare prompted.

"It's just that…"

"You're torn."

"Yes," Brett admitted.

Clare finished her glass of wine. As she picked up

the bottle, she confessed, "And me."

"But we have to make a decision."

While she filled both of their glasses to the brim, she said, "Yes, we do."

Brett stretched his arm towards her across the table and said, "You'd make a terrific girlfriend."

Looking at his big open hand, Clare put down the bottle and then shifted her gaze to his face.

In his office, Big John congratulated Brett and Clare. Then he said, "In your report Louise comes over smelling like a saint so it's your call, Brett. Do I keep her or put her back on the beat where she deserves to be?" Hastily, he added, "Don't answer too quickly. If she goes back on the beat, I might be able to arrange a seriously good deal with Thames Valley. I could get Dennis Kosler to transfer up here and work with you instead." With a wide grin he asked, "So, who's it to be? Jenson or Kosler?"

"As decisions go, that's hardly a tough one."

"OK. Decided. You've got Louise Jenson. Change can be very good for us. It keeps us on our toes. She's your new partner, Brett."

Brett and Clare glanced at each other and then turned to John with puzzled faces.

"That's right," he announced. "This morning you two are looking more cosy with each other than ever so I'm splitting you up. Putting a bit of distance between you won't hurt a bit. You're going to tackle your next few cases separately."